I must venture

again to the World of the Green Star, where, in the body of another man, I had lived the most perilous and fantastic adventures in all the annals of human experience.

I *must* . . . and there was nothing I left behind me on Earth that I could not do without.

Why did I hesitate—why did I linger? Every fiber of my being yearned to drift through that world-encompassing forest of sky-tall trees, where a delicate and ancient people dwelt in precarious balance between implacable foes and ferocious monsters. Where cities of sparkling gems soared from the trunks and branches that sprung miles into a misty sky shot through with sunbeams of mingled jade and gold . . . a world of unearthly beauty and superhuman mystery, where my heart had, at last, come home.

I had nothing to lose by going,
except my life.

"Janchan hurled the bowl of liquid fire."

When the GREEN STAR CALLS

by
LIN CARTER

Illustrated by
Luis Dominguez

DAW BOOKS, INC.
DONALD A. WOLLHEIM, PUBLISHER

1301 Avenue of the Americas
New York, N. Y.   10019

FIRST PRINTING, JULY 1973

1 2 3 4 5 6 7 8 9

PRINTED IN U.S.A.

For Scott Bizar,
who also likes an
old-fashioned yarn.

Table of Contents

PART IV THE BOOK OF JANCHAN OF PHAOLON

PART V THE BOOK OF KLYGON THE ASSASSIN

LIST OF ILLUSTRATIONS

Part 1

THE BOOK
OF KARN
THE HUNTER

Chapter 1

THE VOICE FROM BEYOND

Night after night, I heard that strange and inward call. It sang deep within me, as I tossed and turned, striving to sleep. It called and beckoned within my troubled dreams.

From the night sky it came. From the wintry dark, where cold stars blazed like ice-blue diamonds strewn upon black velvet. From the depths of space itself ... from the farthest corner of the universe ... where a Green Star flamed and a weird world hung amid the void.

Like some siren, calling from the dark and silent abyss between the stars, it sang. Exquisite and pure was the crystalline music of that siren's song. It pulled at my heart; it sang within my very brain.

Only I alone, of all men, could hear the luring music of that voice calling from beyond; for only I, of all men, had voyaged thither, swift as disembodied thought, to that far and fantastic world of marvel and mystery. There, upon that strange world of eternal mists, of titanic trees and jewel-box cities, I had been born anew in the body of a gigantic warrior of legend. Together, he and I had embarked on the strangest adventure ever told, had ventured deep into the mist-veiled world, had loved and lost the most beautiful of princesses.

He had died, there on the World of the Green Star.

I—I had been drawn back across the star-spaces, to my empty envelope of flesh, to the world of my birth.

I was nearly dead when they aroused me from my trance-like slumbers. For too long had my wandering spirit been absent from my slumbering body. Almost had the dark gates of Death opened to receive me ... but not quite.

For I still lived; but never could I return.

13

For weeks the doctors hovered about me, thrusting their needles deep into my veins, helping me to regain my withered strength, my exhausted vitality. During the enforced leisure of my long convalescence I passed the weary hours setting down in my journal an account of the marvels and mysteries I had witnessed on my journey to the Green Star, and the perilous adventures I had survived on that cloud-enveloped world of strange monsters and even stranger men.

Now, at last, they pronounced me fit and whole again. Or as fit and whole as any man may be, who has been confined to his wheelchair, a hopeless cripple since childhood.

The narrative of my explorations and exploits on the World of the Green Star I have locked away in a secret vault. No eye but mine shall ever look upon it until after my death; then the vault may be opened, the narrative brought to light—and the world may make of it what it will.

The savants will scoff at its fantastic marvels, and denounce it as the ravings of a lunatic. The men of science will put it down as an amateur's venture into extravagant fiction; men of sanity and logic will ascribe its origin to the cravings of a helpless cripple to play the part of a man of action, if only on the written page.

The world may think what it likes of my tale. Only I shall ever know the truth of it, and the beauty of Niamh, Princess of Phaolon, whom I wooed and won in the body of another man, and in his name.

I do not mean ever to return to the Green Star; there is nothing for me to go back to. Nothing but futility and pain and sorrow . . . sorrow of broken dreams, the pain of a lost love, the futility of striving for that which cannot be regained.

Yet night after night . . . *I hear the Green Star call!*

Sometimes I ask myself, why did I record that narrative of my strange adventures on a distant world, since I mean never to voyage there again?

Perhaps it is, simply, that I wished to preserve the memory of those weird, unearthly experiences, before they began to fade from my memory—their brilliant colors dimming, like the fresh hues of a withering flower. I wanted to record it all as I remembered it, the awe and beauty, the strangeness and terror, the marvelous adventure only I had lived.

But now I am not sure: it may well be that to relive the marvels and mysteries of my venture into the unknown was a symbolic return to the Green Star—a voyage into memory, to retrace the voyage through space that I have sworn never to perform again.

My reasons are complex and illogical. But, after all, I am only a man. Logic is cold argument in matters of the human heart.

The trouble, quite simply, is this: I had ventured to the World of the Green Star, a disembodied spirit, and thereon had found a body awaiting my coming—or the coming of some other spirit from the vast deep. That body I entered, slipping into it as a hand enters a waiting glove. And thus I assumed the body and name and identity of a mighty hero of the mythic past, the great warrior Chong, whose spirit had been severed from its body by the malignant spells of an envious magician and cast away to drift forever among the nameless stars.

In that body I had loved the Princess of Phaolon— Niamh the Fair—and she had returned my love!

For love of her I had been thrust into a thousand perils, battling terrific monsters and wicked men to protect the flowerlike beauty who went ever at my side.

But in the end I had betrayed the child-woman I loved. I had failed of her trust, there at the last. Trapped among the outlaws of the sky-tall trees, helpless to face the wrath of the Amazon girl, Siona, I had been struck down in the hour of ultimate peril. *And I had died, there on the World of the Green Star* ... leaving my princess helpless and alone amid a thousand terrors, hunted on all sides by merciless and ruthless enemies ... while my sad soul went drifting back to the body it had left behind, on the planet of its birth!

How could I return to that far world again—and for what reason? To float, a disembodied spirit, in homage before the tomb of the girl I loved? Or to look on, helplessly, as she struggled against dangers and foes against which my hovering spirit was but a wisp of air?

These things were undeniably true—yet reason and sanity and logic are poor solace for a tormented heart. By day the memory of my lost love haunted my waking hours

. . . and by night, the Green Star called like a siren through my dreams. . . .

Life on the planet of my birth held little to interest me. True, I am young and handsome, and wealthy—as most men measure wealth. The first is an accident of heredity, the second a matter of inheritance—neither have anything to do with me.

Crippled with polio as a child, in the years before the perfection of the Salk vaccine, I could live out my years in comfortable boredom, surrounded by every luxury that money can buy. The fortune of my father, the country estate of my family, these both are mine to enjoy. But I chafe against the weary futility of this life of cushioned ease; I yearn to be thrust into the wilderness, pitting my strength and courage and cunning against a thousand perils. For only in such moments have I found life worth living.

I was born for the life of wandering adventure . . . but fate chained me to the body of a hopeless cripple.

It was this longing for escape that first drove me to pursue the curious art the Oriental sages call *eckankar*—soul-travel—the liberation of the astral body. The secrets of that lost art were set down in Old Uighur in a strange and precious book written immeasurable ages before Narmer the Lion welded the Two Lands together under one crown, and Egypt was born.

With the resources of vast wealth mine to draw upon at will, I commissioned agents to scour the East for any trace of that age-lost and world-forgotten book. Seven years and two hundred thousand dollars later, it was found in an obscure, minor lamasery. Lost in the confusion when the Dalai Lama and his court fled the invading Red Chinese for refuge in India, the ancient codex had gone astray.

But wealth can open many a long-closed door. And thus, at last, the mysterious *Kan Chan Ga* came into my hands. In those parchment pages, a prehistoric sage had set down the occult wisdom of a forgotten civilization . . . with time, I made that wisdom mine.

Now that I had again regained the strength of body, mind, and soul, I hungered to taste the ecstacy of astral flight again . . . yearned for the intoxicating freedom to venture into far places, a drifting, invisible spirit!

Perhaps only one crippled as I am, can fully understand the intolerable lust for that freedom. One who, like me, has not taken a step since he was six years old, without mechanical aids. One who will never walk the world in this life, in this body . . . save through the timeless magic science locked in the cryptic pages of the *Kan Chan Ga*.

Day after day, I fought against that hunger.

Night after night, the Green Star called from the starry deeps!

And so it came to pass that, one winter's night, I could resist no longer the summons of the Green Star.

I pretended to myself that I would merely venture upon this world . . . to see the Coliseum by moonlight, the Sphinx by dawn, the Taj Mahal under the brilliant noon.

I prepared myself for the adventure.

My suite is in a private wing of the old house in Connecticut that has borne my family's name since 1790. Many is the time I have locked myself in my rooms for days on end, busy with my books, the servants forbidden to disturb my solitude.

This time should be no different.

My precautions taken, my housekeeper informed to avoid disturbing me on any pretext, I stretched out upon my bed and composed my limbs as if for slumber.

I emptied my mind of all trivial thoughts by the recitation of certain *mantras*. Closing my eyes, I visualized an ebon sphere, and fixed my attention upon it unwaveringly.

Gradually, so complete was my inner concentration, I lost all sense of my body.

All outer sensation faded. My extremities became numb. My chest rose and fell as I deliberately breathed shallowly, and slowed my heartbeat by an effort of disciplined will.

I was now in a self-induced state of light trance.

Fixing my attention upon that black sphere, I now saw that it was not a material globe at all, but the circular entrance of a dark, unlit tunnel.

Into the mouth of that tunnel I fell.

Utter darkness swallowed me.

Deeper and deeper I descended into that black tunnel. At length, after an inestimable period of time, I perceived a minute flicker of light beneath me.

It was the light at the end of the tunnel.

I emerged from the darkness . . . and found myself floating in a dreamlike haze of unearthly silver radiance and absolute blackness.

For a long, wondering moment, I stared about myself.

For a moment I could not recognize my weird surroundings.

Then it came across my mind like a flash that what I looked upon was a broad, sloping lawn, mantled in new-fallen snow, and the jeweled blackness of a midnight sky, arching above me.

Looking past the snowy expanse, I saw a great old house of rugged fieldstone, with tall towers and a peaked roof.

The house was my own.

I seemed to be floating sixty or seventy feet above the Earth, weightless as a gust of air.

From a gemmed black sky, wherein the silver rondure of a full moon blazed with glacial splendor, snow fell in shimmering flakes through an utter stillness.

The snowflakes fell . . . *through me!*

And then I knew my soul was free.

Chapter 2

THE THING ON THE MOON

Above, like a great jewel pinned to the breast of night, the full moon glowed with unearthly silver light.

A bodiless spirit, I could travel where I willed, swift as thought itself, faster than any beam of light.

To the moon itself, if I wished.

The thought entranced me. The moon glowed down like a staring and hypnotic eye. Men of my race had trod those cindery plains, and now would tread there no more. The last Apollo flight had departed from Taurus-Littrow and a chapter of history had closed . . . for our era, at least.

So the commentators said.

But I could prove them wrong, if I so willed.

The wish was father to the act. Even as the thought occurred to me, it seemed that I soared skyward at incredible velocity. The snowscape fell away beneath me, laced with black woods and webbed with spidery-thin lines that were highways, and jeweled, here and there, by the dwindling light-clusters that were towns.

Earth fell away beneath me until it transformed itself into a tremendous globe, sheathed in midnight. A diamond-glitter flickered; an arc of light circled the east. Then the daylight terminator blazed up in a dazzle of sunlight and I watched a dawn still hours in the future travel slowly across the Atlantic Ocean, an orb of incredible flame mirrored on a shield of burning gold.

I turned my vision skyward, and saw the moon.

Very beautiful it was, the immense face peering down at me as if puzzled to see a drifting spirit afloat on the soundless ether.

I ascended very high above the Earth.

I was not conscious of the slightest sensation. A man in

my place would be a frozen corpse in the hundredth part
of a second, the breath exploding from his lungs to freeze
into a diamond-mist of ice particles. But I felt neither cold
nor the need to breathe.

Those sensations I had left behind in my body, which
slept in a trance many thousands of miles away, in a
night-shrouded place called Connecticut.

And I—I was free! Free to span the very universe in a
twinkling, if I wished!

Now the moon expanded before me, filling the horizon
like a tremendous bowl. No more did I ascend skyward;
now it seemed that I floated down into a colossal plain of
glittering cracked glass, where a huge, black-ringed crater
glared like a sightless eye.

The crater must have been miles across: the rays of
sheeted glass that extended from it were like frozen rivers,
flashing in the blinding sun.

Toward the black-ringed crater I descended.

And a moment later I seemed to stand in a great valley.
To all sides, the horizon was ringed in by a jagged but circular and unbroken wall.

I looked down. The floor of the crater was naked rock,
with a dull metallic sheen. It was littered with crumbling
fragments of debris, and pockmarked with many craterlets, dozens, perhaps hundreds.

These differed in size from pits you could hide a Cadil-
lac in, to small, circular holes only an inch or two across.
The floor of the crater looked like a flat surface of heavy,
slick mud upon which scattered raindrops had fallen—and
the mud had then been frozen forever, preserving the impact craters.

The debris that lay tumbled about consisted of shards
and fragments of broken rock—doubtless hurled about by
whatever had scored the flat plain with those miniature
craterlets; a meteor shower, I guessed.

The silence was unearthly.

Here there was no air, no rain, no snow. Nothing but
the pitiless glare of eternal day, relieved by the transient
darkness of eclipse, when the Earth passed between moon
and sun.

Like a homeless ghost in Dante's Inferno, I roamed the
floor of this hell of frozen stone and glaring stars.

And then I came upon a wonder.

It was set in the stone floor of the crater-plain. It soared ten or a dozen feet into the sky.

It was a pillar of iron.

Struck with awe, I drifted closer to look upon this marvel with the eyeless vision of the spirit I now was.

The metal thing was about two feet in diameter, as nearly as I could judge with the eye alone, having nothing of known size nearby against which to measure it.

The iron pillar was perfectly rounded and burnished smooth. I call it iron for want of a better word; a dark, blue-black metal, very reflective. If it was not iron, then I can put no name to the metal which composed it.

It was no freak of nature, this shining column of metal that thrust up against the flaring stars. Such perfection of rondure, such straightness, could not have been natural by any stretch of the imagination.

This was the work of man.

Peering closer, I saw the sides of the column were incised with narrow rows of cryptic letters. Strange, hooked characters they were, and like no Terrene alphabet of the many known to me.

If anything, they resembled Sanskrit.

I wondered whose hand had set this thing here, and for what unguessable purpose.

And what was the meaning of the inscription?

Were these the annals of a race unknown, star-wandering visitors from another solar system, envoys from the dim red spark of distant Mars?

Or had some prehistoric civilization of Earth's forgotten dawn traversed the silent abyss between the worlds? Had some crystal vehicle from elder Mu drifted here before the birth of time, or some primal astronaut from lost Atlantis, risen through the seething mists of the Pleistocene, to dare the depths of space,

There was no answer I could put to these questions.

The iron column may have stood here a million years or more, bearing mute testimony to some vanished race that had been the first to voyage between the planets.

In the perfect vacuum of the moon's surface, iron would stand eternal and unrusting, durable for eternity.

Were these mysterious inscriptions the imperishable chronicles of Mars in her prime, or a lost book from Atlantis? Was this message a greeting, flung across the aeons, or a timeless warning of some cosmic danger?

Absurdly, I thought of a "no trespassing" sign, such as Earthly farmers affix to tree or fence-post. Was the pillar of iron a warning to the men of my world that this satellite fell within the borders of some interplanetary empire?

Or was it, perhaps, a gravestone—the marker of some fallen king or hero of the Tertiary—inscribed with the record of his deeds?

Many, I knew, are the mysteries of time and space. Man has yet encountered but a few.

The Gupcha Lama—seventh of the "living gods" of Tibet—he who had translated the mysterious pages of the *Kan Chan Ga* into English for me, on my promise to deliver the priceless original codex to the Dalai Lama when the task was done, had confided to me many things during our peculiar friendship.

He had told me of one certain very ancient lamasery in a forgotten corner of Tibet, called Quanguptoy. There for a thousand years and more successive generations of mystery-priests had studied an age-old science by which pure thought can be made to traverse immensities of space.

The Quanguptoy lamasery had for centuries exchanged wisdom and knowledge with the strange denizens of far-off worlds, he confided. With a white, crawling, fungoid intelligence that dwelt on the twilight zone of tiny Mercury. With a sentient crystalloid entity who inhabited one of the lesser moons of Saturn. With a forgotten race of Insect Philosophers who once had lived in the moon's core but died when the last oxygen reserves were exhausted—and who thrust their immaterial minds forth into the remote future, to assume the bodies of a post-human race of segmented arthropods who will inherit the Earth in One Hundred Million A.D.

The telepathic lamas had devoted a thousand years to the projection of thought, and from many distant worlds and strange beings had compiled a history of the universe itself.

An entity of living gas, who dwelt beyond the galaxy near the surface of a dead, wandering star, told them of the future, which it had explored by the sheer power of mind alone. Told them of man's eventual extinction in an Age of Ice due in twenty-five thousand years; told them how the surviving remnant of mankind would migrate to Sirius and Tau Ceti from subterranean citadels, as Earth's core-heat failed at last, guttering to darkness in the thirtieth century of the Ice Age. Told them how the first visitors from the young planets of Alpha Draconis, come flown hither in crude rocketships of indestructible crystal, would puzzle over the indecipherable mysteries of ruined New York and drowned Chicago and lava-sealed San Francisco, when at last the glaciers receded.

Strange beyond the dreams of science fiction are the unplumbed mysteries of the universe!

There is a wizard who dwells on a dead world about Antares, in a dome of imperishable glass built above a mighty chasm wherein scarlet horrors slither hungrily. The last of his race he is, and that race sprung from the reptiles as we are sprung from the great apes. It is his peculiar curse that he is eternal and deathless, having in a rash moment immortalized himself. He has outlived the extinction of all his kind, and will live on until the energy-death of the universe itself, when the galaxy slows and comes apart, and the stars go out, one by one.

I turned from the iron enigma that stood against the stars, and drifted on my solitary way.

Perhaps no eye but mine would ever scan those rows of unreadable hieroglyphs. The mystery of the thing on the moon might never be solved.

I left it, thrusting up against the starry sky.

And in that sky—the Green Star blazed!

I saw it lift beyond the naked, fang-like peaks of the dead cold lunar horizon.

I knew it at once, with an instinctive recognition I can neither justify nor explain. And my heart leaped within me at the sight of that spark of emerald flame. For on that far world lay my destiny, my triumph—or my doom.

Whatever jest of mocking gods had spun the tangled skein of my days had woven into the woof a thread of jeweled green. Like it or not, my fate was inextricably involved with the fate of the distant folk who dwelt on that far world.

And all at once a longing surged within my soul to visit again that weird world of many marvels. This desire was all but irresistible, and in its rising flood were swept away all of my wise and cautious arguments.

I must venture again to the World of the Green Star, where, in the body of another man, I had lived the most perilous and fantastic adventures in all the annals of human experience.

I *must* . . . and there was nothing I left behind me on Earth that I could not do without.

Why did I hesitate—why did I linger? Every fiber of my being yearned to drift through that world-encompassing forest of sky-tall trees, where a delicate and ancient people dwelt in precarious balance between implacable foes and ferocious monsters. Where cities of sparkling gems soared from the crotches of branches that sprung miles into a misty sky shot through with sunbeams of mingled jade and gold . . . a world of unearthly beauty and superhuman mystery, where my heart had, at last, come home.

I had nothing to lose by going, except my life.

And I placed little enough value on that, God knows. . . .

Chapter 3

INTO THE UNKNOWN

One last glance I cast behind me at the world on which I had been born. I said my silent farewells to her green hills and dim forests and shining seas, to the people I had known and loved, to familiar places and moments that would live in memory. My regrets were few, for most of the memories were bitter. But there were certain things I put behind me now that it would sadden me never to know again ... the taste of a fresh spring morning in the woods of Connecticut; the familiar feel of an old, much-read, long-loved book; the portrait of my mother, smiling, lovely, forever youthful with the immortality of the painter's art, that hung above the mantle in the dining room; the carefully-tended grave of a great, lovable Newfoundland who had been the faithful companion of my childhood....

These things I might never look upon again.

I made them my farewells.

Then I looked beyond the white-flecked azure sphere of the Earth to that place in the eternal blackness of the heavens where the Green Star blazed like a beacon-fire against the dark.

And I left my world behind forever.

Somehow I knew that I would not return again to that strong but crippled body that slept in an unbreakable trance in the dark room of the old house that had been home to my people for a little less than two hundred years. How I could be certain of this I could not say. But the inner conviction was very strong.

Staring into the black sky with the eyes of my spirit-body, I willed myself to the Green Star with all the force of will I had learned from my patient study of the old book from Tibet.

And the dead surface of the moon fell away beneath me—dwindled to a shining mote that hung beside a shrinking sphere of glittering blue—and vanished into the darkness between the stars.

The transition was timeless. That is, I was not aware of any lapse of time. My second flight to the Green Star, like my first, may have taken a moment—or a century. There was no way to measure the interval.

I have come to feel that a sense of the passing of time is an illusion of the flesh, not an absolute universal standard. The wise men of Lhasa teach that both time and space—the sense of distance and of interval—are delusions imposed upon the spirit which is imprisoned in a human body. They teach that to the liberated soul there is only the eternal and the infinite: no bounds, no limits, an endless Now ... and an uncircumscribed Everywhere. As to the truth of this, I really cannot say. But I suspect that, in this as in certain other things, the timeless wisdom of the East has attained to an insight denied the little men of the West who huddle in narrow laboratories, probing at the secrets of the universe with narrow minds, minds too small to contain the measureless Truth.

There was no sensation of motion.

I was momentarily aware of an infinite darkness closing about me. The icy breath of a supernal cold touched the center of my being. The stars blurred ... and *shifted.* ...

And the Green Star blazed up before me in all the glory of her tremendous dawn!

It was a spectacle such as few eyes could ever have seen. The star-strewn vastness of space was filled with a vast sphere of intolerable emerald flame. Thundering gouts of incandescent spume, like a fiery vapor of jade, blazed up from the shimmering surface of the immense orb ... floated in arcs of unendurable brilliance against the dark ... and sank again into the green furnace of the tremendous sun.

I stared enthralled upon the scene. How it was that I could look upon this cataclysmic vision of wonder and might I cannot explain. Had I been a fleshly visitor, my organs of vision would have been blinded in the first microsecond. As an invisible and bodiless spirit, it seems to me that I employed the eyes of my astral senses, but this is only a guess. However it was that an immaterial form can sense the vibrations of light—*I saw*. It is but one of the many enigmas of the bodiless state, and the solution of it I must leave to wiser men than I.

Circling this sphere of cold green fire I spied a smaller globe, sheathed in impenetrable silver mists. This was the world whereon I had ventured in the person of Chong the Mighty ... and how my heart sprang with joy now that I beheld it again!

I directed the flight of my spirit toward it.

Nacreous, dawn-struck mists swirled up around me: for a long moment I sank through mists of turbulent vapors of spun silver, irradiated with fiery emerald.

Then the mists dispersed about me and whipped away, and I looked upon a landscape such as Earthly eyes have never beheld before my coming.

It was a world of Brobdingnagian trees. In their countless tens of thousands they marched from horizon to mist-bound horizon, and most of them were as tall as Everest. Mountain-thick boles sprung from unseen depths beneath to fling their towering spires against the green-and-silver sky. Enormous branches sprouted from the soaring trunks, branches as broad as six-lane highways, bearing up immense clouds of leafage. These leaves were as huge as the sails of ships, and were like gold tissue struck through with sun.

It was an awesome spectacle; once seen it could never be forgotten. Earth affords no mightier, more impressive landscape.

Through the maze of intertwining branches I floated down as lightly as a drifting leaf.

Branches thrust about me now in every direction. Here and there a scarlet reptile clung with sucker-feet to the rough bark surface. An immense dragonfly shot past me, his wings of sheeted opal flashed suddenly with jeweled splendor as he transected a shaft of green-gold sunlight. I could see about half a mile in every direction ... beyond that limit, branches and masses of aureate leafage blocked my vision.

I gazed down: the trunks of the colossal trees dwindled away beneath me like the shafts of skyscrapers, their bases lost in the dense gloom that reigned eternal at the forest's floor.

I did not have even the slightest idea where I was. And it suddenly came to me that in this mysterious world of ti-

tan forests, one tree looks very like another. On my earlier
trip here, I had been lucky enough to stumble upon the
site of Phaolon, Jewel City of Niamh, through pure
chance. Now, unless the Gods of Luck were with me, I
had not the slightest chance of finding it again. Nor, for
that matter, of finding the Secret City of the Outlaws,
where I had taken my last look at the princess, and where,
in the body of Chong the Mighty, I had been slain.

Phaolon or the Secret City might be on the next
branch—or ten thousand miles away! I floated for a time,
musing on this problem, realizing it was hopelessly insoluble.

Princess Niamh and I had been in the act of making
our escape from the outlaw encampment of Siona the
Huntress. The Amazon girl, who had foolishly conceived
an unreciprocated passion for me, had been on the point
of delivering the princess into the hands of certain envoys
from her rival city of Ardha. We had fought our way out
of Siona's fortress to the *zaiph* pens. In that battle I had
received my death wound and had fallen; but my last
glimpse of Niamh was as she fled from the outlaw city,
mounted on a fleet-winged *zaiph.*

Had she safely eluded her pursuers, or had the outlaws
recaptured her? Had Siona sold her into the bondage of
her Ardhanese enemies, or kept her prisoner to wreak
upon the helpless princess her own jealous vengeance? Or
had she indeed made her escape—in which case she might
have found her way back to the Jewel City. Or had she
fallen prey to the monstrous predators who roamed the
world of the mighty trees? Or did she still wander, lost
and alone, searching for the way back to Phaolon?

To have known the answer to any of these questions
would have satisfied me. But it gnawed at my heart that I
knew nothing of her fate for sure. And, myself completely
lost, there seemed no way I could find the answers I so
desperately desired.

For an immeasurable time I drifted aimlessly through
the giant forest, searching for any sign of intelligent life. It
tortured me to think that the girl I sought might be, quite
literally, *anywhere* . . . on the next branch, or in the next
tree, or on the other side of the planet, for all I knew.

And then, quite suddenly, I came upon a tense scene.

By sheerest accident, I had stumbled into the last act of a small, pitiful tragedy.

Four stakes of strange, glassy metal had been driven deep into the broad upper surface of one great tree-branch.

Bound spread-eagled between these stakes, a half-naked boy lay within inches of death. They had bound his wrists and ankles with cruel rawhide thongs to these stakes, stretching out his limbs to their limit, and left him there to die.

And death approached him now on silent, scuttling feet.

At first, the youth did not spy the monster as it stealthily crept near. He was straining every muscle and sinew in a last effort to free one hand from his bonds. Already the cruel thongs had bitten deep into his wrist: his hand was purple and swollen, and red blood dribbled from the tips of his numb fingers. The pain must have been excruciating, but, sinking his teeth into his lower lip, the brave boy struggled on. He would, I somehow knew, continue that struggle to the very last.

He looked to be sixteen, perhaps younger. His lean, bony physique was naked except for battered boots and a scrap of cloth twisted about his loins. Whoever he was, and however he had come to this end, he had been starved and brutally mistreated. The raw weals of a savage whipping gleamed wetly across his chest and shoulders, and his bony ribs thrust through his skin.

His silky hair of raw pale gold was shaggy and unkempt. His face was dirty and sullen, but it was a good face, with clear alert eyes, amber-gold in a tawny-skinned face. He had a strong jaw and finely molded mouth, and his broad, high brow denoted intelligence and breeding.

I could see about him none of the dainty effeminacy I found so offensive in the pampered princelings who dwelt in the jeweled cities. Starved to skin and bones, his limbs were supple and lithe and his muscular development was extraordinary for a boy of his age. He was no painted and perfumed fop from the delicate life of court and city, but a hardy, rangy, long-legged youngster sprung from the savage wilderness itself. I wondered what foes had staked him here to die, and for what reason. And I admired the grim, dogged determination he displayed, as he fought to free his hand from the tight thongs, stoically ignoring the pain he so obviously suffered.

But death was very near him now, in the form of a hideous monster insect. I recognized it as a *phuol*, a sort of scorpion—but one the size of a full-grown dog. Eyes mounted on protruding stalks glared at the bound youth; pincer-like claws swung from an armored thorax; a horrible barbed tail, poison sac swollen with venom, hovered menacingly above its scuttling body as it inched forward on six jointed legs.

The boy had not seen it yet. His full attention was fixed on the thong he was striving to loosen from his puffed, purple hand.

In a way, the thing was beautiful. Its chitinous exoskeleton glittered like blue enamel. Its huge pincers were like something carved from immense fragments of flashing sapphire crystal by some nightmarish sculptor. Eyes like ruby chips blazed with soulless hunger.

Silent as a moving shadow, the blue death glided nearer—nearer.

There was nothing that I could do. I was as immaterial as a wisp of air; I could not even utter a warning cry.

The boy saw it at last. His face whitened, his eyes stared in horror, his lips parted in a cry inaudible to me.

Then, in a rush, the scuttling horror was upon him, the poison-sting sinking its barb in the flesh of his leg.

Chapter 4

THE DEAD CITY

In fascinated horror I watched the last act of the drama. An invisible spectator, unable to intervene, I looked on as the brave boy fought against death.

His cries must have rung loudly through the leafy silence. He threshed his bare body violently, striving to dislodge the venomous *phuol*.

Startled, the monster scorpion retreated from his threshing prey and hesitated before launching a second attack.

The brute would not have long to wait. Poison from its sting had already entered the boy's body and must be infiltrating his blood even now. The lips of the wound blackened almost visibly, and the boy's calf began to swell as the poison circulated.

I knew something of the nature of the *phuol*, although on my previous adventure I had been lucky enough not to encounter one. But the foresters of Siona's band, and the assassins of Ardha, employ the venom of these blue scorpions to render poisonous their dagger-blades and arrow-tips. And I understood that the *phuol* were cowardly killers, who injected their venom into their prey, waited until the poison had paralyzed them, and then fed on the helpless and still-living bodies of their victims.

Already the boy's extremities must be numbing as the subtle venom worked through his system. His eyes glazed; his breath came in ragged, uneven pants; his blond head lolled on one shoulder.

The *phuol* crept stealthily near again.

But this time its charge was interrupted.

Without the slightest warning there stepped from behind the cover of immense gold-tissue leaves a tall, lean man curiously armed with a rod of crystal.

His figure was gaunt, his features ascetic. A close-fitting

"Without warning, there stepped from behind the leaves a tall, lean man."

cowl covered his head, leaving only his face bare. It was a cryptic mask, that face: hooded eyes of lambent mercury observed the scene with cool, thoughtful, unhurried appraisal. The face was the mellow ivory hue of old parchment, youthful and unlined, calm and serene. Keen intelligence and weary boredom gleamed in those brilliant quicksilver eyes: the man had about him the look of the scholar, the aesthete.

One hand was strangely gloved in a black metallic fabric. It was the hand which clasped that shaft of sparkling crystal. This scepter-like rod bore caps of black metal at either terminus. Within the transparent substance of the rod, fierce light quivered and writhed like a living thing.

At his entrance upon the scene, the *phuol* had paused to assess this intruder. Now the blue horror began his creeping advance on the pinioned boy again, evidently assuming the tall man would not intervene.

But the monster was mistaken.

With a swift gesture the cowled man leveled the crystal shaft at the *phuol* and removed the metal capping one end.

Lightning flared! A crackling bolt of incandescent blue-white fire lanced through the green dimness of the branch. Caught in the electric discharge, the giant scorpion stiffened—convulsed—fell to one side, crisped and blackening. Its hideous sting struck blindly again and again at empty air as the monster writhed in its death-throes.

The magician capped his wand swiftly; prisoned lightnings flickered within the crystal shaft as he sheathed this peculiar weapon in a rubbery black tube which hung at his girdle.

Then, ignoring the dying insect, he knelt swiftly by the boy and severed the thongs which bound him to the stakes. The boy sagged limply, staring up at his enigmatic savior with dimming eyes. The magician laid one hand on his naked breast to test his heartbeat; then from a capacious pouch he withdrew a small flask of sparkling red fluid, uncapped it, and poured the contents in the boy's mouth.

Again he tested the heartbeat, and took the pulse of the boy's uninjured wrist. Then, apparently satisfied, he picked up the boy in his arms and strode off into the mass of leafage from which he had emerged.

If any reader ever peruses this narrative of marvels, he will understand how they mystified me at the time. Curious, I sent my spirit floating after the enigmatic rescuer and his limp young burden. I followed them down the slope of a long branch to where a most remarkable vehicle stood parked.

It looked for all the world like a child's sled, with its curled up-curved prow and long, flat runners. It was nearly ten feet long, and the curled prow was shielded to either side with a curved transparent pane like a windshield. The thing was either fashioned of silvery metal, or enameled in that color.

The cowled man stepped into this peculiar craft and deposited his still-living burden in the rear, strapping him in. Then he stretched out in the fore part and did something to a control element under the curved prow. To my astonishment the sled glided off the branch and floated through the air, swiftly vanishing into the distance.

I was filled with amazement. This was the first example of a superior technology I had yet encountered on the World of the Green Star. Most of the Laonese—as the people of this planet term their race—seem to inhabit a cultural level comparable to the High Renaissance. But this remarkable flying vehicle—and, come to think of it, the electrical weapon with which the magician had slain the giant scorpion—suggested that there dwelt upon this world some who had attained to an advanced technology.

Recovering from my amazement, I directed my bodiless flight in the direction the sky-sled had flown. Soon I caught up with the aerial vehicle and could observe it in motion. There was no discharge of vapor or visible energy from the rear of the miniature craft, nor did I see any evidence of propellers. The motive power was a puzzle to me; much later I learned that the sky-sled rode the magnetic currents generated by the planteary magnetosphere, but at the time the power that propelled the vehicle was a mystery to me.

So swiftly did the sky-sled traverse the forest way that within mere minutes it achieved its goal.

And I looked upon an awesome spectacle.

Within the enormous crotch of one gigantic tree, was a city built of black crystal.

It rose in successive tiers, the upper works somehow anchored to the bole of the tree itself, the lower levels extending out upon the level upper surface of the branch.

With the exception of the Secret City, the only other

Laonese metropolis I had seen had been Phaolon itself, that sparkling capital that was fashioned of glittering gems and crystals.

This city was ebon-black in structure, and, although fashioned like Phaolon from crystals, these were dead and lusterless.

The city itself was dead.

How old it was I have no way of telling. But time had broken down its balustrades and toppled many of its soaring spires. Great cracks ran zigzag through the swelling domes and the narrow, crooked streets were littered with fallen shards.

And so it was that I first looked upon the Dead City of Sotaspra.

Not all life was extinct within the ruined metropolis, however. Life still clung to a few slender spires, guttering low like a windblown candle.

Toward one of these towers, somewhat more remote than the others, the magician directed his uncanny aerial contrivance, floating to a landing on the upmost tier.

Unseen, a drifting ghost from a distant star, I followed.

The tower toward which the cowled magician directed the sky-sled differed in several ways from the other structures. For one thing, whereas they were dead and blackly lusterless, this spire shimmered with brilliant color. As scarlet as new-shed blood it gleamed—a graceful, tapering shaft of smooth crystalline substance that seemed cast all in one piece, for all that I could see. At least, no segmentation or jointure could be discerned.

Toward this Scarlet Pylon the sky-sled flew. Hovering like a winged *zaiph*, it floated to a landing upon the topmost tier. I perceived that the Pylon was apart from the others, built on the utmost verge of the Dead City, where the levels rose from the crotch of the enormous branch, ascending partway up the slope of the giant tree-trunk itself.

One spire that blazed and flashed with color, amid a crumbling metropolis of dead black. The thought crossed my mind that this structure had been somehow revitalized—energized—whereas the black, lusterless, ruined towers had slumped into decay, their stores of energy vitiated. I was, much later, to realize that my first impression was strictly true and accurate.

The magician bore the unconscious boy from his craft

into the Scarlet Pylon. Entering a spacious apartment, he
deposited his burden on a couch of sumptuous silken stuffs
and set about without further ado to lance the boy's swollen and discolored leg. Draining off the poison, he cleansed
and treated the wound with swift, economical motions,
smearing the bite with a sparkling salve permeated with
flecks of radiance.

Then he momentarily left the suite, returning with a peculiar apparatus like a tall floor lamp. The luminiferous element of this instrument was a coil of milky crystal,
shielded in a hooded cone of glistening white metal which
shaped and directed the rays.

He affixed this instrument to the floor, adjusted the ex-
tensible shaft so that the luminiferous coil was swiveled to
bring is rays to bear directly upon the boy's injured leg.
He then switched the lamp on. A dim rosy light bathed
the boy's flesh. I gathered that this roseate light was a
form of energy that worked on the cellular structure, ac-
celerating the natural rate of growth.

Leaving the unconscious boy beneath the ruby rays of
the healing lamp, the magician strode swiftly from the
room. In a few moments he returned with a tray of various instruments and stoppered bottles whose employment
obviously pertained to the healing arts. These he utilized
over the next two hours in what I observed to be a vain
and futile attempt to save the life of the boy.

A sympathetic audience, albeit an invisible one, I lingered in the chamber. Something in the dogged determination with which the boy had battled for life aroused my
admiration.

With the aid of an apparatus which consisted of a tangled maze of glass tubes, the cowled man succeeded in
draining most of the venom from the boy's bloodstream.
The healing ruby rays enormously accelerated the healing
of the wound, and a poultice of glittering crystalline salts
reduced the swelling and, I assume, fought infection.

But it would seem the magician's fight against death
was to be a hopeless struggle. Too much time had elapsed
between the attack of the scorpion and the time the boy
was brought into the Pylon laboratorium. The poison had
largely accomplished its deadly purpose; the boy would
not live through the night.

Unless an unknown and inscrutable fate intervened.

Night fell over the World of the Green Star. As day waned, the boy's life waned with it. Paper-white, dripping with perspiration, he lay on the couch surrounded with healing instruments. I gathered from the expression on the cowled man's face that the boy's heartbreat grew ever fainter, and I could see that his breathing grew difficult. Toward the middle of night his condition worsened. His breast rose and fell almost imperceptibly now, as his breathing became more shallow.

The magician had done all that lay within the scope of his art. At length, he shrugged, switched off the apparatus, and left the apartment, abandoning the youth to his fate.

I hovered nearby, observing to the last this little drama into which chance had thrust me.

Then, toward morning, I saw an amazing sight.

It was as if a drifting whorl of luminous vapor rose slowly from the boy's motionless body.

In the dimness of the half-lit chamber, the mysterious vapor glowed with a wan and pearly luminescence.

It seeped slowly from his flesh, floated for a brief time above his body, melting into empty air.

I sensed, with a thrill of uncanny awe, that I was observing the dissipation of his vital energy. How it came that the strange phenomenon was visible to me, I cannot precisely explain. Perhaps it was due to my bodiless state. An invisible spirit myself, perhaps I saw with the eyes of a spirit, to whom another spirit is dimly visible.

Near dawn an intense point of brilliant light seemed to emerge from the boy's breast. Starlike, a focused point of pure flame, limpidly white, it seemed to float up from his body . . . hung above the motionless corpse for an instant . . . then drifted out of the room. And I knew that it had been given to me to observe an immortal soul leave its mansion of clay.

The boy was dead now. Still warm, his flesh would soon cool, the rich red blood congeal in his veins, his limbs stiffen in the grip of rigor mortis.

I think a madness came over me then.

What impelled me to this act I cannot say: it was no conscious act performed of my own volition.

But, swift as thought, I drifted down into the empty, warm, and waiting body!

Chapter 5

I LIVE AGAIN

My flesh was at once numb—and on fire. A sound like surf roared in my ears. My lungs fought for air, struggling against a vast weight that seemed piled upon my chest.

It came to me, then, what a mad thing I had done, entering the vacated body of the forest boy. For the body had been at the very point of death, and I, who had died once before in the flesh of Chong, knew that death was a trauma as shattering to the psyche as birth is said to be.

But I fought, clinging to life. Red mist gathered before my eyes. Excruciating torment flayed through my nerves as pulse and respiration began anew. Had I possessed the strength, I would have shrieked aloud with the pain: but I had not breath enough to do so much as whimper.

After an endless time, the torment lessened. The red mist cleared from my vision and the roar of my blood moving through the inner ear faded.

To draw each breath was a struggle against enormous odds. My heart labored violently within my chest, battling for life. My consciousness faded as the powerful life-instinct took over control of the battle against death.

And I swooned or slept.

After an unknown interval, I struggled back to wakefulness again to gaze up into the cool, aloof eyes of the cowled magician who was regarding me with surprise and slight admiration. Above the muffled thunder of my struggling heart I could not make out the words he murmured as he spoke to me. He lifted my head and set a beaker to my parched lips. I drank down a potent, stinging beverage as effervescent as vintage champagne, as bracing as a tonic. The fluid bit my tongue and slid down my throat to form a center of warmth deep within me, from which waves of languid heat expanded through my extremities. The numbness faded almost magically from my flesh, and the agony of the poison ebbed. And I swooned or slept again.

For days thereafter I lingered, half-conscious, clinging to life. Gradually my hold strengthened, and I sensed myself no longer in danger of losing my precarious grip on life or my rash tenancy in this new body.

I slept much, while strange lights beat upon my flesh and curious potions circulated through my veins. Doubtless my mysterious savior kept me drugged much of the time with some narcotic.

Why I lived while the boy himself had died I cannot say for certain. Perhaps it was simply that I am a full-grown man, with a greater store of vigor and life force, while he was a skinny, mistreated, half-starved stripling. At any rate, I recovered in time from the effects of the sting of the *phuol*. The wound on my leg healed; the poison-rotted flesh reknit. At first I could only hobble; in time I limped; but before very long I could walk or run as good as ever.

That I lived anew in the body of another did not trouble me. The boy died and there had been nothing that I could do, in my bodiless state, to help him. When the soul has fled, the empty body is dead matter. Had I not entered it as a wandering spirit and revitalized it, the body would have decayed, its elements returning to the matrix of nature from which it had sprung.

But my tenancy of this body was a strange and unique experience for two reasons. It was not that merely to inhabit a borrowed body was new to me, for I had known the phenomenon before, on my first visit to the World of the Green Star. Then I had dwelt in the body of Kyr Chong, the Lord Chong, whose spirit had been torn from his flesh and driven forth to wander forever among the stars by a hostile enchanter. The memories of Chong had long-since faded from his body's brain, and other than an extraordinary ease and facility in learning the Laonese language, my tenancy of his flesh had occasioned no peculiarities.

But the body of this boy was very newly dead—if indeed his body can be said to have died at all, since I entered it at the very moment his spirit fled forth. In the case of the boy, his brain was still a living organ and all his memories were still fresh. Thus, for example, I knew his name, which was Karn—or "Karn the Hunter," as he

thought of himself. And I knew that he was an orphan
lad, his family long-since slain by the monstrous predators
of the wild, who lived alone among the giant trees, subsist-
ing on the game he slew with bow or lance, or trapped in
cunningly contrived nets. There were many such as the
boy Karn who dwelt apart from the treetop cities amid
the wilderness of the giant trees. Sometimes they banded
together into tribes of small clans, but as often as not they
dwelt alone and apart, living off the forest, eschewing the
companionship of their own kind.

Life for such persons is hard, for the World of the
Green Star is a savage wilderness—an ocean teeming with
enemies, in which there exist only a few islands of civilization and safety.

Thus it had been for Karn the Hunter. And there was
still fresh in his memory the moment of his capture by a
hostile tribe from which his own parents had fled into exile before his birth.

It was an uncanny thing, to delve into the alien memories of another person and another life. But my curiosity
was, I think, natural enough under the circumstances.
Thus I searched into the memories of Karn the Hunter,
and thus I learned of the circumstances which had led him
to that grim scene in which I had first encountered him,
bound to the death stakes, set out to die under the venomous sting of the scorpion monster. . . .

His father had been named Athgar, and he had been a
hunter of the Red Dragon nation, a tribe of wandering
savages who roamed among the giant trees at eternal en-
mity with all others of their kind. Athgar the Hunter had
seen and had fallen in love with the girl Dioma, the
daughter of a chieftain. His love had been returned, for she
had often looked upon him from afar, admiring his
prowess in the hunt, his fearlessness in battle, his stalwart
body, and his nobility of features and deportment.

Thus they met and thus they loved. But her father had
promised her to another, and refused Athgar when he
came to sue for her hand. Athgar's rival for the affections
of Dioma had driven him into exile on the pretext that he
had boken taboo, but on the fateful day of the nuptial
rites, when Dioma was to have been delivered into the
arms of the rival chieftain, Athgar appeared, slew his

rival, and carried off into the wilderness the woman he loved, who became the mother of Karn.

As I have already stated, life among the giant trees is hard. It is especially hard for a lone man, encumbered by a woman and a newborn child. In time, both Athgar and Dioma succumbed to the countless perils of the wild, leaving the child Karn to live or die on his own.

But Karn the Hunter had not died. The blood of mighty warriors and of many ancient chieftains ran in his veins, and his young body swelled with sleek thews: in time, if he survived, he would grow into a tall and majestic warrior like his father, fit to bear up the standard of the Red Dragon nation in war, and to lead a mighty party in the hunt. And Karn survived—for, although still but a boy, he had inherited much of his father's fearlessness and dogged determination, as he had his inches and his brave prowess and courage.

But the cruel laws of survival in the wilderness impose the sentence of unending warfare upon those who choose to live apart from their fellow men, or those who are driven into the lonely life. Rogues and outlaws, they are, for the most part, and to be slain whenever they are encountered.

Such had been the doom of Karn the Hunter, the son of Athgar the Hunter; for in time he had been captured by Red Dragon scouts from his father's own people. They had imprisoned him, starved and beaten him, and staked him out to die a merciless and lingering death under the poisonous sting of the *phuol*.

It was an irony of fate. For the savage boy had survived in the wild forest where a city-nurtured child would have succumbed to the thousand predators who roamed the wilderness. These perils he had survived—only to fall prey to his father's foes, to his own people, who had staked him out to die on a branch whereon the venomous *phuol* make their nest. And from this grim jest of fate the hooded savant had saved him, for some idle whim or perhaps a deeper purpose which as yet remained unknown.

As for Karn's mysterious savior, he was a cold, aloof, impersonal man who had not as yet divulged his reason for rescuing the wild boy from the scorpion monster. His name was Sarchimus, and in this chronicle I have referred to him as a "magician," for want of a more fitting term. Sarchimus the Wise was he called, and in this Scarlet Pylon he dwelt alone, insofar as I had learned as yet. There were others like Sarchimus, who lived here and there in various portions of the Dead City, but it was to be some time before I encountered any of them.

Sarchimus was silent and inscrutable; he lived apart and busied himself in curious studies whereof I knew but little, for I seldom saw him. Although he was solicitous to me while my wound knit and my body healed and I recovered my strength and health, he was neither my friend nor my master. The mystery of Sarchimus was one I had yet to solve.

And so this first peculiarity of my new embodied state was that I now possessed the living memories of another: I shared his memories only, and not his being or his sense of identity, for that had fled into the Unknown with his immortal spirit. The other peculiarity of which I have spoken is the strangeness of my new body, which was that of an immature boy. For I had been a full-grown man in my former life on the planet Earth far away, and to find myself a boy again was weird and unsettling, and it took me a considerable time to adjust to my new condition.

My own boyhood on Earth had been cruelly curtailed, for since I was a child of six I had been crippled with polio and had not taken a single step without mechanical aids. So now, to the strangeness of my new immaturity, was added the strangeness of dwelling within a strong and athletic body. A body that yearned to run and climb and play with the reckless abandon of a healthy boy—a body that chafed at restraints and conditions and ill health. It was all rather like a strange dream.

To be a boy again—and a healthy one, at that—was a dream that many men have had. The actuality of the dream was, oddly enough, uncomfortable. For one thing, although my spirit was that of a man, my emotions and my self-control were immature and tentative. On those rare occasions when I saw my keeper, or owner, or whatever he was, I suffered from the awkward, blushing self-consciousness of a tongue-tied boy. Far from being able to deal with him on a man to man basis, I felt very much in awe of his superior wisdom and mysterious accomplishments, and knew myself to be his junior and not at all his equal. But these emotions and feelings were those of the boy Karn, not those of the man-spirit which now inhabited his body; it was, however, to be quite some time before I became—*myself*—and accepted my new life as Karn the Hunter.

The Pylon of Sarchimus was large and capacious. The magician or savant, or whatever I should call him, dwelt in his own private apartments into which I was forbidden to enter, and thus I saw very little of him, once my wound was healed and my health restored. He was a cryptic man, my "master," and left me to my own devices most of the time. He seemed to care nothing for my company and generally ignored my very presence, and certainly demanded nothing from me in the way of service—at first, anyway.

I cared little, and did not bother to puzzle into his mysteries. It was enough to me during this period that he neither abused nor mistreated me in any way, which was a lucky thing. For I had not yet managed to fully master the savage instincts of Karn the Hunter; and Karn was, by ancestry and birth and self-training, a savage warrior and a killer.

Sarchimus, as I say, left me to my own devices, and sometimes I did not even glimpse him from a distance for days on end. His enigma was insoluble. When I had lain weak and helpless, he had tended me with the gentle solicitude of a kindly nurse; once my wound was healed and I was able to be up and around on my own, he left me to myself very largely, never required my presence, and hardly ever talked to me.

We ate apart and lived apart, my master and I. The mysterious people who had built this city had mastered the strange secrets of an alien science. I will have more to say on this subject later, but for the moment let me remark that one of their most remarkable scientific attainments was in the preservation of food. They had known a technique for instantly preserving food and it was upon these supplies of perfectly preserved nutriment that my master and I subsisted. Each apartment in the Scarlet Pylon contained a certain niche in one wall, protected by a panel. When this panel was opened, a switch caused a variety of foods encased in transparent cubes to revolve past the eye of the beholder in a recess. Roast meats and stews and all manner of vegetables and fruits, pastries and deserts, and a considerable variety of unfamiliar beverages, were on display in this manner, all in a condition of perfect preservation. Having chosen the repast you desired, pressure on a certain switch caused the transparent cube containing the food of your choice to be detached from the continuous sequence of stacked cubes. The cubes themselves were easily unsealed and when this was done the food or drink you had chosen was before you—steaming hot or cool and frosted, ready to be devoured. The supplies of these preserved foods set aside by the Ancients, as I soon came to think of them, seemed virtually infinite in variety and number. Thus, although I suffered something from loneliness, I would never go hungry for as long as I remained a guest—or a prisoner—in the Scarlet Pylon of Sarchimus the Wise.

Part 2

THE BOOK
OF SARCHIMUS
THE WISE

Chapter 6

THE SCARLET PYLON

To the eyes of the boy Karn, all of his surroundings were mysteries and he regarded his new mode of life, with its many remarkable conveniences, with superstitious awe. This seemed only natural, for the savage boy had lived alone in the wild under the most primitive circumstances and had never known anything remotely like city life before.

I, however, as an Earthman from Twentieth Century America, could realize the remarkable and sophisticated scientific accomplishments which had been attained by the mysterious folk who had built this city. And I was busily putting two and two together.

The man who had saved Karn the Hunter from the fangs of the deadly *phuol* was a seeker after wisdom, a quester of lost secrets. He seemed a youngish man, as far as I could tell, for his features were unwrinkled and his brow smooth—but, as I have elsewhere remarked, it is oddly difficult to ascertain with any particular degree of certainty the age of any of the inhabitants of this World of the Green Star. This is due, I think, largely to the curious fact that the Laonese seldom think of time as we Americans think of it, and hardly mark its passage. We Americans, you know, are extraordinarily conscious of the passing of time: we cut it up into hours and minutes and seconds, and wear small but very complicated machines on our wrists so that we may be almost constantly aware of the flow of these time-divisions, which are purely imaginary and invented by ourselves.

We also have the odd custom of marking time into larger and yet larger divisions—days and nights, weeks and months, years and decades and generations and centuries and ages—and have devised all manner of methods

by which to observe the passage of the "moment called
now" through these ever-widening divisions. Calendars,
almanacs, and history books are only a few of our inven-
tions designed for this purpose. But the Laonese know little of this curious custom of hours; they hardly even think
in terms of decades, much less of years, and hence it is remarkably difficult to ascertain the ages of any of them.
For they themselves cannot easily tell how old they are—
it is a question they never ask, and something they seem
never to think about, or very rarely.

Thus, although I possessed the full memories of Karn
the Hunter, I cannot really say with any exactitude just
how old he was when first I entered his untenanted flesh.
From the looks of his body, I could have guessed him to
be an adolescent. A boy of sixteen, perhaps, or seven-
teen—long-legged and a bit scrawny, ribs showing through
his bare bronzed hide, with awkward hands and feet. Sev-
enteen was the mental estimate I formed of his—of *my*
age.

But as for Sarchimus the Wise, he might have been a
man of anywhere from the middle thirties to a well-
preserved and youthfully agile fifty; further than that I
could not even guess. He seemed to be about in his early
forties—but I am only guessing.

How long he had lived here in the Scarlet Pylon I never
knew. He was a sober, thoughtful man—an intellectual,
virtually a sage or a philosopher—and something of a
combination of magician and scientist. There were, as I
soon came to suspect, other savants of his mysterious calling who shared the deserted and ruined metropolis with
us, but these he thought of as rivals and enemies, and they
dwelt apart from each other in scrupulously maintained
privacy in what amounted to nothing less than a state of
continuously alert armed truce.

But more on this subject later.

He was a somber, solemn, incommunicative man, this
Sarchimus my master, and I saw little of him once my
convalescence was done and I had regained my health to
such a degree as to be able to get around by myself and to
tend to my own needs. Aloof and inscrutable, dwelling far
apart from my own quarters in apartments of his own, we
had little or nothing to do with each other, at least in the
beginning. And while the boy Karn could not help feeling
a tingle of superstitious awe and primal fear in the

presence of the mysterious "magician"—as he thought of Sarchimus—I, a civilized American, thought of him as a sort of scientist or scholar and was eager to converse with him on an equal level as an adult. For I understood at least the rudiments of the science I saw about me, and would have questioned him from a level of scientific knowledge that would probably have startled him and aroused his suspicions—for such advanced knowledge would have surprised him, coming from an untutored wild boy of the forest.

For this reason, then, it is perhaps well that I saw so little of him and that our paths crossed but seldom.

The Dead City of Sotaspra in which the science magician had made his home had been emptied or abandoned ages before, as could have been guessed by the extent of its decay. But obviously, in its prime, it had been the cradle of a superior civilization. In fact—as I soon had reason to suspect—the Sotaspran civilization had been a remarkably advanced culture, which had progressed far beyond the present state of the other cities of this planet which I had visited or heard of during my previous venture here. The sky-sled which flew by riding magnetic currents was an example of the heights to which Sotaspran science had attained before its mysterious eclipse, as was the crystal blasting-spear with which Sarchimus had slain the scorpion monster. This particular weapon was called the *zoukar*, by the way.

Sarchimus was not, of course, a Sotaspran by birth, for the city was uninhabited, save by a few seekers after the lost secrets of its ancient people. He had been born and educated in a distant city whose name I never learned, and his thirst for knowledge had drawn him here as it had drawn his fellow-savants. Entering the Dead City of Sotaspra many years before, Sarchimus had sought out the isolated Scarlet Pylon and had made it his home and a closely-guarded fortress. One by one he had excavated from the ruins the various instruments and vehicles of the lost civilization, had subjected them to intensive study, and had in many cases mastered the secret of their use and revitalized them. But many more instruments remained cryptic and unsolved mysteries to him, and many more secrets were still undiscovered.

That I lived at all in this healthy young body was due

entirely to the fact that the healing lamp had been one of the first secrets of the lost science of Sotaspra which he had recovered and mastered. I could not help feeling a certain debt of gratitude to him for thus saving me from an agonizing death, although his reasons for so doing remained unexplained. The impersonal manner in which he regarded me, and the way he remained aloof and apart from me, shunning any closer communion, gave me cause to suspect that his reasons for rescuing Karn the Hunter from death were other than merely altruistic.

At any rate, I had the freedom of the tower, save for certain sections thereof, among which were the private apartments of Sarchimus and his laboratorium, wherein he deposited all his secrets. During the day I was free to come and go as I wished, with few duties which demanded my attention. We ate at different hours, and, although it had been suggested to me that it would be wiser and safer to remain within the Scarlet Pylon itself during the hours of darkness, there were few restrictions placed upon my movements, and little in fact that was actually forbidden me.

As soon as I was able to get around by myself, I began eagerly exploring as much of the Scarlet Pylon as was permitted. I cannot say exactly what I was looking for, but what I desired was some means of ascertaining the position of the Dead City in relation to those few portions of the globe known to me from my former incarnation on this planet as Kyr Chong. I suppose I was unconsciously looking for the Laonese equivalent of a map or atlas or geography book; but whether or not the Sotasprans had actually possessed anything of this nature I could not be certain. There was, you see, no way I could find my path back to where I had left the Princess Niamh unless I could discover where the Dead City was located in relation to the Secret City of the Outlaws. At the very least, I hoped to find the location of Niamh's city, Phaolon. When last word had come to me of Phaolon, the Jewel City had been in imminent danger of siege by the legions of Ardha, a hostile city. Even if I was unable to find my princess, I could still be of service to her if I could assist in the defense of her kingdom.

Alas, the Sotaspran civilization seemed not to possess maps or atlases. Or, if indeed there were such, they were either not to be found in the Pylon of Sarchimus, or were somehow concealed from random discovery.

Over a period of many days I searched as much of the Pylon of Sarchimus as was not explicitly forbidden to me. Sloping ramps connected the twenty tiers of the crystalline spire, and a veritable labyrinth of apartments, antechambers, and cubicles were to be found on the several floors. Although the tower had either survived the decay of the Dead City in a remarkable state of preservation, or had been thoroughly and laboriously refurbished, few of the various suites were at all furnished and most gaped empty as if abandoned.

The librarium of Sarchimus occupied most of one entire floor. Here, curving walls were lined with shelves which were cumbered by a profusion of folios and librams and volumes of many sizes and description. Never before in my wanderings upon the World of the Green Star had I seen such a collection of books, and had my search been motivated by mere idle curiosity, I could have spent many days happily engaged in exploring this universe of alien literature. As it was, I was eager to be gone from here, anxious to discover some notion of the whereabouts of this city, and fearful to display too obvious an interest in the librarium, which, had he at all noticed it, would perhaps have aroused the suspicions of my master. A savage boy from the wilderness, after all, should not know how to read.

The kind of books made by the Laonese tend toward immense folios. They are very heavy, measuring two or three feet across, and in order to peruse them in comfort you require the services of a lectern. Merely moving them one at a time is a task of considerable labor, and thus, for these reasons, my search of the library of the Ancients was cursory, furtive, and hasty. Moreover, I was ill-equipped for the study of Laonese literature; my education into the language had largely been on the vocal level. Although I had received some tutoring into the written script at the hands of Khin-nom, the old philosopher of Phaolon had been supremely concerned to acquaint me with the spoken language, not the written.

Even from my cursory search, I gained some notion as to the contents of the vast librarium, and learned nothing of what I sought. Most of the volumes were tomes of a metaphysical nature, pondering the verities of the universe, and composed in a language so highly technical or symbolic as to be virtually incomprehensible. I found few books devoted in any degree to the physical sciences—and wondered thereat. For how had Sarchimus managed to find the key to the lost science magic of the Ancients, without a text?

Some of the tiers of the tower were devoted to understandable uses, such as sleeping apartments and the vast librarium. There were also galleries and arcades given over to collections of artifacts. The immense sophistication of the Ancients was visible in their art as it was in their remarkable technology; for here were mosaics and frescoes which would not have looked out of place in Terrene museums devoted to the avant-garde—geometrical abstractions, pure studies in tonal values, nonobjective works in which meaningless organic shapes of color contrasted subtly with each other.

But other art works, perhaps dating from an earlier and less intellectual era, were representational in nature, although seemingly allegorical in theme. These invariably depicted a race of winged beings whom I at first assumed to depict angels or genii.

While some apartments of the Scarlet Pylon were devoted to obvious uses, others were enigmatic and mysterious. For what conceivable use, for example, had the Ancients constructed that central shaft that ran from the bottom of the tower to its utmost crest? A mere hollow tube it was, with sliding panels that opened onto each and every floor of the tower. I wondered if it could be something in the nature of an elevator shaft; as it lacked either car or cables, I soon abandoned this thesis, and simply set it down as yet another in a world of many mysteries.

Some of the suites Sarchimus had reserved for his own uses. There was an immense laboratorium filled with crystal vats and sparkling tubework, wherein he spent a considerable portion of each day. Another lengthy hall was filled with gleaming machines of unfamiliar design and unknown purpose. And there was also a circular rotunda wherein abstract shapes of solid crystal stood on plinths of copper, jade, and iron. Lights moved and shimmered through these masses of shaped crystal, each differing from the other. One towering ovoid contained an inner structure of minute and starlike points of light which flickered from light to dark in a complex rhythm all their own—for all the world like a string of Christmas tree lights draped about an invisible armature!

Another bulbed crystal glowed with a sourceless aura of dim radiance that pulsed slowly in throbbing rhythm, like the beating of a gigantic heart somehow rendered visible rather than audible. And there was also a soaring, curved shaft which seemed to contain captive lightnings, for long crackling sparks of blue-white fire, intolerably brilliant, searing to the eye, sped randomly from top to bottom of the monolith.

The purpose of this rotunda of irradiated crystals was just one more mystery.

But there were greater mysteries to come!

At length I came into an enormous hall of many levels; that is, curved balconies, three in number, encircled a vast open space three full stories in depth.

This was one of the unrefurbished portions of the Scarlet Pylon, and it was one of the strangest areas I had yet explored. All furniture, draperies, and hangings had been stripped from the circular tiers and the vast floor below—or had perhaps crumbled into dust through the passage of time, for the glimmering pave was strewn most oddly with heaps and mounds and swaths of powdery dust, amid which were small odds and ends of dry and porous wood and morsels of some ceramic substance that resembled potsherds.

Within this vast place were over one hundred statues.

I have remarked on the art works left behind by the extinct Sotasprans earlier in this narrative, and I have mentioned their principal sculptural motif is that of allegorical or mythological figures that are winged, like angels or demons. Well, all of the immense number of statues wherewith this enormous room was thronged were in the likeness of these remarkable winged genii, or whatever they were. They stood about seven feet tall and were depicted in a variety of amazing tasks—amazing not because of the unusual nature of the tasks, but of the extremely commonplace nature of them!

That is, some were pictured as sitting—although there was no furniture for them to sit upon—while others leaned against walls or columns. A dozen or so had been carved as if they were leaning on their forearms against the balustrades of the upper balconies, staring down into the vast hall beneath. More than a few had been sculpted in a recumbent posture, as if they were supposed to be sprawled about or stretched out on divans or couches. These lay flat on the floor amid mounds of dust and decaying wood.

It was all most remarkable. I have never before seen a sculpture gallery composed of figures designed in such lifelike detail, depicted in some ordinary and mundane occupations. They were, also, carved from a most peculiar substance, like white chalk, which seemed to my untutored eye an unlikely substance for sculpture, as the lightest blow could break away an elbow or a finger; in fact, many of the figures, particularly those depicted as stretched out on nonexistent couches, were broken.

It was merely another mystery.

But one I was later to remember. . . .

Chapter 7

THE CITY OF MONSTERS

If I have given the impression that I had no commerce with my master during this period, let me correct it here. Although for the most part Sarchimus left me to my own devices, busying himself with abstruse researches and experimentations which required privacy, I was occasionally summoned to attend him and from time to time performed small services for him, such as the running of errands.

The first of these meetings came at the terminus of my period of convalescence, when the science magician demonstrated to me how to use the automatic food machines and the sanitary conveniences. During that interview he also gave me to understand the limits that he imposed upon my movements. I could go where I wished, save for those rooms whose portals were sealed with the mark of the Hand, these being and these I was to consider as his private domain; any intrusion would be at peril of his ill will. This insignia, by the way, denoted Sarchimus himself and was in the nature of an heraldic blazon—the mark of a human palm, with fingers widespread, in crimson. This was the seal of Sarchimus.

During this first interview I was given to understand that to attempt to leave the Pylon by any egress was to imperil my life; the bottommost seven tiers of the Scarlet Pylon were somehow hostile to humankind, or so it was explained to me. I was not long in discovering the truth of this in my own way.

My search for some manner of map or atlas of the World of the Green Star had soon exhausted all of the chambers of the tower, save for those sealed with the

Scarlet Hand and the lower seven tiers of the structure itself.

One day I decided to descend by the series of sloping ramps and explore the base of the Scarlet Pylon. I think I disregarded the warnings of Sarchimus as an attempt to hold me prisoner through superstitious fear. I think I can also explain my rashness in venture to ignore his warnings as the actions of a restless and reckless boy—for at this point I had not yet managed to establish an inner balance between my youthful body and juvenile emotions and the sober maturity of my intellect and spirit.

I found the seventh tier a dark and gloomy place, the floors littered with rubbish, the walls covered with green mold. The air here was not only dead and vitiated but also steamy and rank with vile odors, like the foul miasma that rises from the scummed waters of a swamp.

On the sixth floor I found—horror!

It was darker here than on the floor above, and the floor underfoot was carpeted with slimy mosses. Huge fungoid structures rose about me as I crept cautiously down the ramp—bloated and unhealthy fungi of enormous size, glazed with putrescent moisture, splotched with huge discolorations.

As I stepped to the bottom of the ramp my ankle was caught suddenly in a tenacious grip. I voiced a cry of astonishment and struggled to free myself. But the most violent contortions failed to loosen my foot from the green and furry tentacle that had ensnared me.

I had earlier found a scalpel-like implement of transparent metal in one of the cupboards of the suites above, which I had secreted about my person under the abbreviated tunic the science magician had given me to wear—an effeminate, silky thing, colored a repulsive lavender, which left my brown legs bare to the upper thigh. Now I snatched the glassy blade from its hiding place and slashed at the ropy tendril which wound ever tighter about my foot. The blade sawed through the ropy substance as through a vine, and to my surprise and consternation the thing that gripped my foot bled *greenly*—like sap from a living branch!

In a moment I had freed myself from the clinging tendril. As I kicked loose from its clutches, I got a good look at it for the first time. It was hard to make out in the dim green gloom, but the thing which wriggled and writhed across the mossy carpet for all the world like some manner of serpent was—I now realized with horror—a species of vegetable life, no reptile at all!

It was, in fact, a vine—complete with a hairy cilia of rootlets, twigs, and even flowers!

As it threshed madly about, shedding green, sap-like gore, I perceived other such vegetable horrors slithering toward it from the further aisles of the fungi grove. In an instant they had coiled about their injured fellow, insinuating their bristling rootlets into its open wound, and clung to it, feeding like vegetable vampires.

Thus I escaped without harm from my first experience with the dread crawler-vines.

Circling the place where the vine monsters lay entangled, feeding gluttonously on the vegetable gore of their fallen fellow, I continued my cautious descent of the Scarlet Pylon.

I knew now that the warnings given to me by Sarchimus were neither idle nor fallacious. But such was my determination, that I refused to turn back. With a wary eye out for more of the slithering vines, I prowled the aisles of bloated and enormous fungi, located a descending ramp thickly and loathsomely carpeted with grisly mold, and cautiously followed it down to the fifth tier.

Here there existed a mere ghost of light—a dim aura of corruption that flickered about the nodding heads of the swollen fungi.

Here, too, I found horror beyond belief.

A vast bulk shouldered through the stalked fungi and blundered toward me. It was an oddly unformed creature, shaped rather like an immense worm, but it progressed in a sort of lumbering charge on several pairs of short, stumpy feet which ended in thick pads. The thing had a heavy, fatty skin or hide which was of a pallid and repulsive hue, sickly yellow banded with white, and was splotched with green-gray mold. Its head was a bulging and featureless mass of fleshy leaves or petals, like cabbage leaves, but thicker and more meaty. It had no visual or auditory organs that I could clearly see, but I saw with a thrill of indescribable horror sprouting from amid the thick, wet petals of its visage *two flowers growing, red and baleful, flowers whose extended and vibrating stamen and pistils seemed to taste the air—swiveling clumsily toward me, as if the flowers were eyes!*

I shrieked and turned to flee, but the lumbering worm-thing was upon me in the same instant. The thick wet pet-als of its face slapped and clutched at me like deformed hands, and I saw that the underside of each petallike flap was lined with prickly thorns. These tore at my flesh, drawing blood, and sunk in, clinging to my bare shoulder and upper arm.

The huge, blundering thing stank of mold and corrup-tion and rotting flowers. It slobbered and fumbled loath-somely at my flesh and, yelling like a demented thing, I struck again and again, driving my glassy scalpel deep into its broad breast. The fatty tissue of its flesh was pulpy and soft, and I carved it into ribbons without finding a vital organ.

Suddenly, I thought of those flowerlike eyes and slashed at them, severing one at the stalk, whereupon the monster squealed and shuddered, its thorny facial petals releasing me so that I fell to my knees in the slimy mosses. One or-gan of sense left unimpaired, however, the vast worm-thing squirmed toward me again in a multilegged rush and would have trampled me underfoot had not a miraculous intervention saved me from my own folly.

For suddenly the green gloom was split apart by a knife of stabbing electric fire!

The fattish breast of the worm-thing exploded, slabs and gobbets of wet tissue splattering about. The stench of ozone was sharp in my nostrils, together with a curious succulent odor my Terrene memory somehow identified as frying mushrooms.

The thing squealed and squirmed and fell on one side, writhing and coiling sluggishly, stumpy feet pawing clum-sily at the air, its breast gouged in a smoking, blackened pit.

I looked up, dazedly, into the solemn, expressionless features of Sarchimus the Wise who stood there, his crys-tal blasting-wand clutched in one hand.

And then I think I fainted.

The magician had entered the lower levels by means of a wall panel which disclosed a lift. He bore me back into the upper tiers and to safety again. I feared his wrath, having disobeyed his instructions, but I suspect that Sar-chimus was a being of pure intellect into whose peculiar mode of existence the emotions had little or no role to play.

"Now, boy, you perceive the wisdom of my counsels, which were not given on mere whim or through intent to deceive, but for your own good," he said gravely.

I nodded humbly, begging his pardon for my violation of his precepts, which was occasioned, or so I told him, through unendurable curiosity and no desire to go against his wishes.

"Very well; this time I will overlook the transgression. But in the future be more careful, and obey my strictures to the letter, for they are derived from sources of information you can know naught of. The lower tiers of this structure are the haunt of terrible monstrosities, as are the streets of the city itself, and the other buildings. You have narrowly escaped from the death-fungus; had you just brushed against it, it would have released a cloud of deadly spores which would cling to the membranes of your throat and lungs, feeding thereupon, and growing until in instants you would have been suffocated. That was on the seventh level. The crawler-vines, a species of vegetable vampire, you have already encountered—but the *saloogs* are the deadliest of all, and you could never have survived the attack, armed only with a knife, for they lack any vital organs whatsoever and are unkillable, save by such weapons as my death-flash," he warned. He indicated the crystal rod capped at both ends with glinting metal, which he bore in his right hand; the hand went gloved in metallic fabric which, I assume, insulated it from contact with the captive lightnings of the *zoukar*.

I questioned him in a faint voice as to the nature of the unkillable brute which had attacked me in the lower levels of the tower, the thing he called a *saloog*, and learned that such beasts are weird half-animal, half-fungoid predators. They roam the deserted and ruin-choked avenues of the Dead City, and like the crawler-vines and the death-fungus and yet other even more horrible brutes, are the hybrid spawn of the city itself, the results of evolution gone mad.

The energy-impregnated crystals whereof the buildings of Sotaspra were constructed more than a million years ago (he told me) fed the mechanisms of the city with an inexhaustible flow of power. But the builders of the city had, in the course of ages, lost all control over the energy crystals, which went wild, their radiations breeding

monstrous hybrid creatures which in time destroyed the
city and slew the Ancients themselves. Although the crystals are long ages dead, the hybrid predators breed still,
for which reason the city is deemed accursed by all civilized races of the World of the Green Star, and only a few
daring savants such as my master himself care to venture
into the City of Monsters to wrest the secrets of a lost
wisdom from the haunt of ravening horror.

Seeing that I had taken no hurt from my experiences,
Sarchimus soon left me to my own thoughts. Now I had
been doubly warned, but from the experience had come
away with valuable information.

I now knew that it would be impossible, or at least very
dangerous, for me to attempt to leave the Scarlet Pylon
on foot.

And I had learned that my master had some subtle
means of keeping unseen watch on all that took place
within the precincts of his tower; for it was some system
of hidden mirrors or camera eyes which had apprised him
of my danger.

I resolved to continue my search, but with greater care
than before.

And the very next day I made a gigantic discovery.

Chapter 8
THE WINGED MEN

By this time I had explored all of the apartments within the Scarlet Pylon, save for the very lowermost tiers and the rooms sealed from my access by the sign of the Scarlet Hand.

And I had begun to piece parts of the puzzle together.

There were many small, mysterious things about the design and decoration and furnishings of the Pylon which intrigued me. A peculiar motif ran through many of the mosaics and frescoes and other artifacts, that of strange winged figures of pallid gold. At first I had dismissed this element in the decorations as being merely allegorical; now I was not so sure. For the Winged Men appeared again and again in the sculpture, the design of furniture, and the wall paintings that ran around the upper portions of so many of the suites. And there was that hollow central shaft whose nature and purpose remained an insoluble enigma.

The science magician had told me, casually and in passing, that the peoples who had built the City of Sotaspra had flourished a million years ago. *One million years ...* an enormous span of time, surely; on the planet of my birth, the ancestors of my race first emerged from brutehood a million years ago. Yet here on the World of the Green Star there had dwelt a people capable of tapping the energy-lattice frozen in solid crystal, able to navigate the atmosphere of their planet in magnetic sleds, and to imprison lightning in wands of artificial manufacture.

Could the Ancients whose secret lore Sarchimus studied have been—*pre-humans?*

Before I could learn further details of this mystery, I must gain entry into those chambers sealed off with the mark of the Scarlet Hand.

And I would only dare that if the science magician himself were to be absent from the Scarlet Pylon for a time.

As things worked out, my opportunity came on the day following my adventure in the lower tiers. Purely by chance I happened to be strolling on one of the ornamental belvederes which overlooked the desolate city. A shadow fell over me from above. Looking up, I saw the sky-sled gliding off through the dim gold-green daylight. The cowled figure of Sarchimus could be seen mounted on the aerial vehicle. Where he was going, or for what purpose, or how long he would be absent—these things I could not know.

But my chance had come.

And I took it!

The laboratorium was of little interest to me. Nor were the sleeping chambers of my master. Yet another red-marked door opened upon a workroom where sheaves of parchment manuscript, scrawled with enigmatic calculations, littered a metal desk. But a further suite opened upon the secret itself!

It was a large, shadowy room with a domed ceiling, the curve of wall and crystal window masked behind heavy drapes.

As I entered a faint sound came to my ears.

I froze motionlessly, listening with taut nerves for a repetition of the slight scraping noise that had come to me. Perhaps it had only been my imagination. . . .

Clasping my glassy knife in one brown fist, I strode forward on silent feet—twitched aside a fold of heavy drapery—

The Winged Man stared back at me solemnly.

He was like one of the carved crystal statues magically vitalized; one of the weird figures in the painted frescoes, suddenly brought to life.

Tall and slim he was, his flesh palely golden, his slender torso and inhumanly elongated limbs devoid of hirsute adornment. His head, with its high, tapering skull, was startlingly alien: strange, yet beautiful in a way. He—for the nude figure was unabashedly masculine in gender—had great, sad eyes set under overhanging brows, and a soaring dome of a skull, hairless as a babe. From the center of the brows curving across the skull to the nape of his neck ran a stiff crest of darkly golden feathers. This verticle ruff stood about six inches high.

The eyes were orbs of mystic purple, luminous and liq-

"The winged man stared back at me solemnly."

uid, and without whites—strikingly inhuman, yet there was
a very human sadness and despondency about them as
they stared solemnly into my own.

The most remarkable thing about him was his wings.
These were folded back and towered high above his shoulders like the wings of a bat. Bat-like in their construction
they were, too, a horny, tough membrane stretched between thin ribs of bone or cartilege. But they were
feathered along the terminus of the membrane . . . and I
saw, peering closer, that what I had at first glance mistaken for bird feathers was a kind of serpent scale, overlapping and convex, like human fingernails set in an overlapping series.

I later learned that it was by means of these curious
hollow scale-feathers that the Winged Man controlled his
flight to an exquisite degree; for the horny feathers permitted him to trim the pitch of his flight for all the world
like the ailerons of Terrestrial aircraft.

The gaunt, golden figure sat hunched on a stool in a
cage of light. An open cube composed of twelve segmented crystal rods composed the angles of this cube, and
from each jewel-like segment a thread of brilliant light
connected to another in a geometric web woven of pure
radiance.

Something warned me not to permit my fingers to touch
that scintillant web. I had extended my hand almost auto-
matically—now, at the voiceless inner warning, I snatched
my hand away. The Winged Man regarded me somberly,
purple eyes haunted with an unspoken sorrow. A strange
thought flashed through me—that the mysterious golden
creature had inserted that flash of warning into my very
mind.

Even as the notion occurred to me, something in the expression of those purple eyes apprised me of the truth of
my assumption.

The Winged Man was telepathic.

On impulse, I strove to communicate with the captive
creature. I strove to make my mind blank and receptive,
to refrain from all thought, so that the vibrations of another brain might resonate through my own being. And in
a moment a cold intelligence spoke within me.

I perceive you to be captive here, even as I, the gaunt,
golden creature said mentally. I fumbled with words, un-
certain as to method.

Speak aloud, if you wish. I will sense the meaning of your words more easily that way. You will observe that the members of my race, the Kaloodha, lack the auditory organs, the creature telepathed again, gesturing with one long-fingered hand at the sides of his head. I saw that he had no ears and that his skull tapered in an unbroken curve to the point of his long jaw. Oddly enough, this did not in any way seem a deformity; somehow it looked "right."

"The—the Kaloodha?" I repeated. The golden creature nodded soberly.

The Kaloodha—the Flying Ones. We preceded mankind on this planet by a million years, but destroyed ourselves through our own unbridled folly. I, Zarqa, am the last living member of my species.

"Why does the science magician hold you prisoner in this cage of light?" I asked. The Winged One regarded me sadly.

So that he may wring from me by his torments the secrets of my vanished people, he replied. *Already, of the Seven Savants, he has become first in his mastery of the ancient wisdom—and all, all, through my unwilling aid.*

At last I knew the secret of Sarchimus the Wise! An actual member of the race which had built the City of Sotaspra was the ultimate source of his achievements in resurrecting the lost science of the Kaloodha!

And I had learned, as well, that six other searchers after the science magic of the Sotasprans shared the Dead City with him. Something of this I had long suspected, and from a remark which Sarchimus had let slip the night before, I had gained unsuspected further proof of my feeling. For I had often noticed, while staring out over the ruined metropolis from one of the balcony-like ornamental belvederes, that while most of the crystalline structures were dead and black and lusterless, a few buildings among them yet gleamed with vital color and living light, as did the Pylon of Sarchimus. Among these were an Opal Spire, a White Dome, and an Azure Minaret. Zarqa informed me that the savants who resided in these revitalized structures were named Hoom, Sarpasht, and Karoeth. These were the chief among the six rivals of Sarchimus the Wise, and of them all, it was Hoom of the Opal Spire who was the most dangerous and the most to be feared. "Hoom of the Many Eyes," he was called; and it was said that little which occurred within the precincts of the Dead City of Sotaspra escaped his cunning notice.

The clue that Sarchimus had let slip, by the way, was that the crystal buildings fed on energy; thus, a building still luminous with color, and thus still powered, was most likely to be the residence of another savant such as Sarchimus himself.

Intrigued, I questioned Zarqa at length. I was puzzled as to how it had come to pass that he was the prisoner of the science magician—and, for that matter, how he still came to be living when the rest of his kind had perished from the hybrid predators a million years before. His answer was that, toward the final extinction of their race, the great brains of the Kaloodha had achieved a method of virtual immortality, whereby they hoped to prolong their lives for untold future ages. This recipe, which Zarqa referred to as the "Elixir of Light," proved dangerous and erratic, and had at times the unexpected side effect of sterilizing males of the race, while it had no effect of any kind on the Kaloodha females. The race thus died out rapidly, not only due to the attack of the hideous plant-animal monstrosities bred by the uncontrolled radiation factor, but because the males, immortal and sterile, outlived the females. Zarqa himself was the final survivor of his kind, and was more than a million years old. He had dwelt here in the Scarlet Pylon, alone with his memories amid the ruins of his people, until the coming of Sarchimus, who discovered him during a period of slumber or aestivation, when he was virtually helpless. I gathered that, to relieve the boredom and monotony of his unending existence, the Winged One periodically fell into a self-induced state akin to hibernation, during which he slept a century or a millennium by.

Further questioning revealed the secret of the amazing white stone statues I had marveled over during my early exploration of the tower. A vital factor in the composition of the Elixir was a certain rare ingredient whose absence causes petrification rather than immortality. Those of the Kaloodha who had unwisely experimented with the incomplete formula were turned to eternal stone!

And thus I became that most miserable of all living beings, the last of my own kind, Zarqa concluded his story. *I am the Last Kalood, and when at length I perish from the mistreatment or the neglect of Sarchimus, then is my glorious race truly extinct. But Sarchimus hopes to doom himself to a similar fate, although he understands it*

*not. For he strives to wring from me the recipe for the
Elixir of Light, whereby he will become as immortal as I.
Thus far I have resisted his importunities as best I could,
but for seven and seventy days now he has denied me the
golden mead which is the nutriment upon which my kind
subsist, and I am greatly weakened and fear I cannot for
very long withstand his urgings.*

"How long can the Kaloodha survive without this
mead?" I asked, and he replied that after one hundred
days of total deprivation a Kalood was usually too weakened and sunken in apathy to respond favorably to the remarkable vivifying powers of the nutritive substance.

The Kaloodha, incidentally, had found they required the
golden mead with all the fervor of addiction. This, too,
was an unsuspected side effect of the immortality process;
prior to their immortalization they had subsisted upon the
usual varieties of nutriment enjoyed by ordinary humans—hence, of course, the supplies of perfectly
preserved foodstuffs available on every tier, upon which
Sarchimus and I had been dining.

*It will be an ill service to the folk of the world, to loose
upon them a Sarchimus made immortal,* he added sadly.
*Already has he forced from me many secrets of weaponry
and stealth and the dealing of death at a distance. But recently I have divulged the mode by which metal automatons may be vitalized and directed by a single will; from
such he can compose an invulnerable army of robots to
overrun the tree cities and to bring all nations of your
kind under his dominance.*

The prospect was horrifying, and the hairs prickled on
my neck at the thought that had I not ventured to violate
the sanctity of those apartments sealed by the Scarlet
Hand I would have gone all-unknowing of the terrible
menace Sarchimus posed to the World of the Green Star.

*But now you must go quickly, and return to those
apartments wherein you are permitted to reside,* the mental voice whispered. *For I detect the approach of the magnetic flux, and deduce that Sarchimus is returning from his
mission.*

I bid the sad-eyed Kalood farewell, promising to aid
him if I could, and replaced the draperies concealing the
force-prison in which the science magician held captive
the million-year-old Winged Man.

Chapter 9

HOOM OF THE MANY EYES

The day which followed, and the day thereafter, Sarchimus was busied in those workrooms and chambers which adjoined the dark hall wherein the gaunt, golden Kalood was imprisoned in a cubicle of intangible energy, so I had no further opportunity to converse with the sad-eyed creature I pitied and whom I had already begun to think of as a potential friend and unexpected ally.

It would seem that what Zarqa had told me was no less than the truth itself. For Sarchimus was engaged in energizing the automatons whereof the Winged Man had spoken. Tall, ungainly things of sparkling brass with featureless visors for faces they were; and the metal automaton that came to clanking life under the hands of Sarchimus was only the first of many. The thing stood seven feet tall, its hands great spiked mauls, and it looked like nothing more than a suit of medieval armor brought to life. Sarchimus paraded the metal monstrosity before me, and I could not repress a shudder of revulsion which he doubtless mistook for superstitious terror.

On the third day after my conversation with the Kalood, there came an unexpected break in the monotony of my internment in the Scarlet Pylon. It was not the first time that Sarchimus had sent me on an errand, but it was the first errand that took me outside of the fortress tower. The goal of my errand was a supply of miniature energy crystals which were concealed in a vault beneath one of the buildings of the city, a trilobed dome which Sarchimus described to me in such minute detail that I could not possibly mistake it. The crystals he required for the vitalization of further automatons, since those crystals already in his store proved too large to fit the mountings.

In preparation for my venture out into the Dead City,

the savant set about the base of my throat a peculiar collar or yoke of some ropy, translucent stuff. This collar fitted snugly, but not too close to interfere with my breathing.

"Now, attend closely to my words, boy," he said in measured tones. "I am sending you forth because I am not able to go myself, since the crop of brain crystals in my breeding vats will attain maturity at any hour and will spoil if I am not at hand to insert them into the skulls of my automatons. But do not think to seize upon this errand as a chance for escape! Know that this collar which I have bound about your throat is a length of Live Rope whose reflexes are attuned to the vibratory emanations of this Pylon. I have adjusted the reflexes to a nicety; you may safely venture as far as the trilobate dome, but to go further from the Pylon will cause the collar to tighten about your throat. It will draw tighter with every *farasang* you journey, and should you go as far as three *farasangs* from the Pylon, the Live Rope will strangle you to death."

He eyed me with a severe expression on his usually serene features. "And do not think to cut the Rope and escape, for the reflex patterns will instinctively convulse the Rope to the point of instant strangulation at the touch of a blade. Do you understand?"

I nodded, affecting a dispiritedness which I did not, in fact, feel. For Sarchimus could not, of course, have known it, but to flee from the Pylon at this time was the matter furthest from my thoughts. I would not have dreamed of escaping without having somehow attempted to release the sad-eyed Kalood from his force-prison.

"But, master," I asked, "how shall I get to the trilobate dome unscathed? For you have told me that the streets and structures of the city are the haunt of terrible monsters, such as the *saloogs*, and of yet other brutes even more fearsome."

He produced a small talisman of multilayered crystal and foil, shaped like a locket.

"Fasten this to your wrist or girdle," he counseled. "It broadcasts an energy wave precisely opposite to the life-force of the plant-animal hybrids, and they will instinctively avoid its proximity. Now begone!"

I descended the lower tiers unmenaced, observing that the savant was correct in his assumption that the wrist-talisman held the hybrids at bay. For crawler-vines writhed frantically from my path and lumbering *saloogs* fled squealing at my approach. The portal of the tower stood ajar, fronting on a street choked with moldering debris all overgrown with peculiar large flowers of a distinctly unwholesome aspect. Their huge, fleshy petals were covered with disklike suckers such as adorn the tentacles of octopuses and there hung about them the stench of rotting offal and decayed meat. Although the cannibal blossoms jerked aside on their segmented stalks as I made my way between them, I did not breathe easily until I had passed them by a wide margin.

The city presented a scene of such decay and desolation as I have never before encountered. Magnificent buildings of superb crystals lay broken and crumbling to every side, their sparkling stones blackened and dead. The streets that wound between the ruined mansions were like a rankly grown jungle, teeming with weird predatory life. The radiations of the crystals had indeed twisted awry the forces of evolution, and to every hand I saw fantastic hybrids of plant and beast such as might have been drawn from the nightmares of Hieronymus Bosch. Birdlike aerial creatures that resembled flying flowers fluttered overhead; trees that bore for fruit mad, glaring eyeballs bent their insane multi-orbed gaze upon me; prowling, hideous, composite monsters of every description avoided my path in terror.

And so I made my way safely down into the central city, glad of the open air again. All about, filling the sky, rose the immense trees of the Green Star World, like arboreal Everests. Shafts of mingled jade and golden sunlight fell through masses of foliage like vast cloud-canopies. Here and there wild *zaiphs* flashed like winged glittering jewels far above me. Somewhere in this mysterious and unexplored wilderness was the exquisite princess whom I loved: but whether alive or dead, whether safely among her people, or imprisoned among her enemies, I could not say....

Without difficulty I entered the trilobate dome and ransacked its crypts for the energy crystals which would vitalize the metal automatons. I found a bin of those of the appropriate size, and filled the knapsacks. I regained the upper street level again without mishap. The collar of Live Rope was firm about my throat but its stricture caused me no discomfort.

Bending my steps back to the Scarlet Tower, I was suddenly accosted by a stranger. He was a mild-faced, smiling man of amazing obesity, gowned in a robe of woven metal which glistened with iridescent hues like a cloth spun of rainbows. Fat men are rare among the Laonese, whose racial type runs to slenderness and a certain effeminate delicacy. Nevertheless, with his wobbling paunch, triple chins, and plump, smiling cheeks, the stranger was Laonese, as his amber skin and lisping speech denoted. He was very bald, and although he resembled nothing so much as a plump, placid Buddha, with an external smile fixed on his lips, I could not help noticing that this mildness did not extend as far as his eyes, for they were cold and shrewd and calculating, like chips of frozen ink.

"Are you not the boy who serves Sarchimus of the Scarlet Pylon?" he inquired in a soft, wheezing voice. I nodded, recognizing him from the descriptions given me by Zarqa.

"I am; and you would be Hoom of the Many Eyes, the arch-rival of my master," I said, which must have surprised him, for he blinked in consternation, and then forced a chuckle.

"Such quickness of mind!" he said admiringly. "My dear colleague has acquired a treasure of perspicacity to assist him in his distinguished labors! But I assure you, my young friend, that the esteemed and worthy Sarchimus and I are but professional competitors, and that our rivalry is devoid of personal rancor."

"That may be," I said evenly, wishing that my master had seen fit to arm me with some weapon—for I doubted not this obese, mild-faced man was about as harmless as a *phuol*, and equally as venomous. "But you delay my return to my master's abode. What is it that you desire of me?"

"To be of service to you, my young friend," he said smilingly. A certain note of pity entered his tones. "For I am in possession of certain information of the greatest value to you, which bears upon your personal safety."

"To what do you refer?" I inquired guardedly.

"My poor young friend, you think me your enemy and Sarchimus your friend, but, permit me to reassure you, the facts are otherwise." He shot me a shrewd, cunning glance, obviously noticing that I was on guard and restive to be gone.

"I know something you do not know," he said softly.

"The reason why your master rescued you from death, and keeps you about him."

I was taken aback. How cleverly had Hoom read me! Of course, this was the one vital morsel of information I lacked; and something on which I had often conjectured.

"And what reason is that?" I asked. He smiled, beaming at me benignly.

"Alas, youth, you have fallen into the hands of a ruthless and inhumane master!" he said, shaking his head dolefully. "Your master experiments with a hazardous medicinal called the Elixir of Light, whose side effects are as dangerous as they are unpredictable. Three captives in his Pylon have already reached their untimely demise during his experimentations; now the cruel and egocentric Sarchimus has arrived at a final formulation, which he intends to test upon your helpless person within mere days. The despicable and treacherous Sarchimus encountered you in the veritable knick of time, for he was down to his last human test-subject when he chanced to discover you staked out for death under the stings of the *phuol*. Should you unfortunately succumb to the unknown effects of the Elixir, he will have left only a certain adventurer from Phaolon the Jewel City, who fell into his clutches some time ago."

A thrill of excitement went through me . . . who could it be, whom the savant held captive? If Hoom spoke the truth, and if a citizen of Phaolon was secreted somewhere within the Scarlet Pylon, he could perchance lead me back to the realm of my lost princess!

I fixed a stern eye upon the fat little man in robes of shimmering opalescence.

"I think you lie, Hoom; for I have searched the tower of my master from base to crest, discovering no human captives."

He shook his head as if bemoaning my distrust of his motives.

"Your suspicions are unfounded, and I regret heartily that you mistake me for a prevaricator! You will find the last of a party of explorers from Phaolon concealed in a wall compartment on the seventeenth tier of your master's edifice, in a soundproof cubicle marked with a symbol—thus and such—which may be opened for view and converse in such-and-such a manner. . . ."

I listened to him closely, reserving my trust until he

should be proved innocent of my suspicions. The mere fact that he knew of the Elixir of Light and its dangerous unpredictability alone partially convinced me; but his motive for apprising me of my present danger was still unclear. I inquired sharply on this point.

"Common humanity, my lad, impels me to this act of simple charity! However, my humane instincts go even further than this, and I am anxious to assist you in escaping from the toils of this cruel and cunning monster who masquerades self-interest behind the guise of altruism. But I fear there is no safety for you, my dear child, until the unscrupulous Sarchimus has met his just deserts. . . ."

"In other words, you suggest I should kill the one who saved my life?" I asked.

He bemoaned my cynicism, but applauded my perceptiveness.

"A fitting end," he observed, "betrayed by one whom he would himself betray!"

I considered the situation thoughtfully, and said: "Well, it's true enough that I wish to escape from the tower. But I need a map of this part of the world, with nearby cities clearly marked, and some method of swift transport—a saddled *zaiph*, perhaps. . . ."

From beneath his robes, Hoom smilingly produced a tightly-rolled scroll of parchment. "I have anticipated your desires," he wheezed, eyes shrewd. "Not for nothing am I called 'Hoom of the Many Eyes'; I have observed your fruitless search of the librarium, deduced that you desire orientation in order to attempt the journey to a friendly kingdom, and have myself prepared a cartographic guide. As for a steed, one is already to hand that is swifter and more tireless than any *zaiph* yet bred: I refer to the aerial contrivance which rides a magnetic flux."

"The sky-sled? But I don't know how to operate it!"

"That, too, I have anticipated, and this document provides clear instruction into the modes of piloting the vehicle," he said.

"What is your price for these gifts?"

He shrugged, spreading both pudgy hands.

"The death of Sarchimus. For too long has he lorded the superiority of his accomplishments over we lesser students of the ancient mystery-science! With the demise of Sarchimus, the worthiest and most intellectual of his competitors can hope to inherit his secrets."

"I gather you refer to yourself." I smiled.

He beamed with smug aplomb, but did not deny it.

"Well, I will accept these documents—as presents, not as bribes," I said finally. "As for slaying my master, well, I will do what has to be done in order to protect myself from treachery; more than that, I cannot promise."

"No more than that is needed," said Hoom of the Many Eyes. "For a youth as perceptive as yourself has doubtless ascertained by pure logic that there is no safety in flight unless he who would pursue is—ah—unable to do so."

I nodded without further words and accepted the map and the instructions to operating the sky-sled. But privately I determined that, rather than commit cold-blooded murder on one who, after all, had rescued me from certain death and nursed me to health again, I would simply free Zarqa and escape in the sky-sled. Since there was only one such vehicle in the Pylon, Sarchimus would be unable to pursue me and my safety was thus insured.

I returned to the Scarlet Pylon with the crystals, my mind busy with plans and conjectures, anxious, first of all, to discover if Hoom had been accurate in stating a Phaolonian prisoner was concealed in the tower. Finding him was the first item on my agenda; flight and freedom, the second.

Chapter 10

JANCHAN OF PHAOLON

There came on the very next day the opportunity for which I waited. The brain crystals had matured in the breeding vats, and the power crystals I had procured on my mission beyond the tower fitted their mountings perfectly; so for the entire day Sarchimus was fully occupied in vitalizing and testing his new army of automatons. Since there were so many of these, he selected the largest single chamber in the Scarlet Pylon for that purpose, said chamber being, of course, the immense hall in which I had earlier discovered the host of white crystalline statues which were, in actuality, the petrified Kaloodha.

Once my master was engaged in this activity, I wasted no time in descending to the seventeenth tier and seeking out the apartment sealed with the Scarlet Hand. I found it a clutter of apparatus of inexplicable design and purpose, but, scrutinizing the walls, I found behind a gorgeous tapestry a panel marked with the small, unobtrusive symbol Hoom had described; operating the catch according to his instructions, I fitted my eye to a small hole thus revealed and peered within.

A young man of noble demeanor and handsome visage reclined on a divan within the secret compartment. From his jeweled trappings I knew him at once for a courtier of Phaolon, although, as it chanced, not one with whom I had become acquainted during my former incarnation at the court of Niamh the Fair.

Below the eyehole was a small speaking-tube into which I spoke. The young man sprang to his feet, staring around in a bewildered fashion.

"Have no fear," I said through the speaking-tube. "I am not your captor, but a captive like yourself. My name is

Karn the Hunter, the son of Athgar, of the Red Dragon nation."

Pressing my ear to the orifice, I discovered I could hear the young man clearly enough.

"I know not where you are concealed," he said in a pleasant baritone, "nor how your voice addresses me from empty air in this manner, but I greet you in comradeship, my fellow captive. I am Prince Janchan of Phaolon, of the House of the Ptolnim."

"How did you come into your present captivity?" I inquired.

"The Princess of Phaolon disappeared on a hunting expedition to observe the Dance of the *Zaiph*," he said. "It is believed that she fell prey to a tree monster, and it remains unknown as to whether she lives or has been slain. But we among her loyal courtiers, knowing her to have vanished in the company of that greathearted hero, the Kyr Chong, believe that a chance exists that she yet lives, and have sworn to search until finding proof positive of her woeful demise. I left the Jewel City in the company of a score of youths of noble or aristocratic birth, all sworn to the quest of the princess. Alas, those who survived the perils of the wild were taken captive by this vile enchanter, who benumbed our senses with a narcotic aroma and who has held us prisoner here for an unguessable period. One by one my brave comrades have vanished from their compartments, to venture to an unknown fate; and of all our company, I fear I alone am left."

My heart beat violently at this report. Well did I know of these events—I who had been the Lord Chong in my previous incarnation on the Green Star World—I who had followed my beloved into peril and who had protected her as best I could from the thousand dangers of the giant trees, until the treacherous blow of a cowardly foe struck me down in the moment of ultimate hazard. Often had we speculated, Niamh and I, while roaming the branches of the mighty trees or enjoying the temporary haven of the Secret City of the Outlaws, that courageous and noble chevaliers of Phaolon were even at that same moment combing the great forest for some trace of our whereabouts. My heart went out to the bold young princeling, Janchan, for his dedication; and I resolved to delay my escape until I should be able to effect his release as well as Zarqa's.

In few and hasty words I told him of the events leading to my own captivity, and of the supposed motives of Sarchimus in holding us, and informed him of the suspected fate of his missing comrades. I also conveyed to him something of my plans for escape, but, upon the attempt, I could find no means of securing entry into the cell wherein he was confined. I searched as long as I dared, without managing to locate a catch or lock, and was eventually forced to abandon my quest. Bidding a hasty adieu to Prince Janchan, I told him I would return for a further try later.

My master Sarchimus was still busied with the vivification of his horde of automatons, who clanked noisily about the enormous hall, bumping into balustrades, clumsily smashing the statue-like forms of the petrified Kaloodha, and getting in each other's way.

Assuming that it would be an hour or so before my master had completed his tasks and had brought the brain crystals of the metal creatures into attunement with the vibrations of his own will, I ventured to the private suite where Zarqa himself was confined within the force-prison. I found the sad-eyed being much the same as on my earlier visit, and hastened to apprise him of the swift march of events. He evinced no surprise at the warnings of Hoom, gloomily admitting he had guessed the savant had captured me so that I could serve his needs as an extra test-subject.

While I have thus far withstood the torments and deprivations he has visited upon me, the gaunt, bewinged Kalood said mentally, *somewhat of the formula for the Elixir is known to Sarchimus. That is, he knows the ingredients—all save one—although he does not know the proportions of the mixture, or the timing and interval and duration of the admixing process. I had not known of the human captives, but had deduced from hints he let fall that he had tested provisional versions of the recipe upon hapless subjects of some kind.*

The Winged Man was unable to be of any material assistance to me in my scheme of escape. He himself was unable to escape from the energy web which held him prisoner, whose lock was attuned to the personality of Sarchimus himself; neither could he explain how to set free the Phaolonian princeling, whose cubicle was doubtless se-

cured in a similar manner. I left after this, promising not
to flee until I had assisted my comrades in misfortune to
escape with me. But how I might work this was still unknown.

That night my master surprised me by an unwonted
display of amiability. He invited me to share his evening
repast in the sumptuous apartments given over to his personal uses. Generally the savant kept quite aloof from my
company, so this gesture of friendly hospitality was quite
unusual. I accepted his invitation to dine with him gratefully; for it might yet prove that he was not so vile and
despicable a villain as the cunning words of Hoom would
make him out to be. On this point I determined to reserve
all judgment.

The dining alcove was a chamber hung with cloth-of-sil-
ver draperies whose glimmering highlights were eerily akin
to the strange quicksilver eyes of Sarchimus himself. My
master was robed in soft purple stuff, and, for this occasion, had set aside his customary cold aloofness of manner; we conversed on a variety of subjects, reclining on
divans drawn up to a metal taboret laden with rare delica-
cies. His manner was, if not actually ingratiating, at least
animated and sympathetic. He questioned me at length
concerning my birth, my former life in the wild, and such
inconsequential matters as childhood diseases and the average state of health my parents had enjoyed.

I found his choice of conversational topics unusual, to
say the least, but set the matter aside as due merely to his
solitary habits, which had given him little experience in social mixing.

The foods were deliciously spiced and mostly unfamiliar
to my palate. The principal beverage was a bitterly chilled
wine likewise unfamiliar, although thoroughly delicious.

After fruit and pastry, Sarchimus invited me to sample a
rare liqueur, and produced a green, effervescent brandy of
extraordinary bouquet. I sipped it cautiously, found it
heady and delicious, and drank it to the lees.

A numbness ran through me; my limbs became leaden;
the empty goblet fell from my nerveless fingers to thud
against the deep-woven carpet.

"What . . ." I gasped. The science magician smiled, his
glittering eyes hooded and unreadable.

I attempted to struggle to my feet, but found myself

"Now, at last, comes the moment I have waited for!"

bound as if with invisible chains to the divan. In a moment I was incapable even of speech and could only lie there, helpless though fully conscious, staring with an expression of astonishment at the savant.

He rose to his feet and approached my couch. Bending over me, he seized me by a handful of my tousled gold mane and pulled my face around so that I was staring directly up into his own. Then he struck me a sharp blow across the mouth. The pain that must have flickered in my eyes seemed to please him, for he smiled slightly.

"Excellent! The drug has caused complete paralysis, with no loss of consciousness, and you are fully capable of experiencing pain. Now, at last, comes the moment I have waited for!"

He picked me up in his arms and strode into an inner chamber, which I saw was outfitted like a chemical laboratorium. Flasks and canisters and quantities of spiral glass tubing littered porcelain tables drawn beneath long windows, heavily draped.

I was completely incapable of speech or movement, and helpless to resist him in the slightest. With rough but impersonal hands he stripped away my tunic, and spread out my naked body on the floor of the chamber in an area bathed with brilliant light from a lamp suspended from the ceiling above. The strangling collar was still clasped about my throat, for he had not seen fit to remove it upon my return from my mission into the Dead City. Now he neutralized its gripping reflexes by a touch from the electrical rod cased against his thigh, stripped the loose, wormlike plastic thing away and tossed it into a corner.

I lay naked, spread-eagled in the pool of merciless light while he bound my wrists and legs to rings of steely glass set in the floor. There seemed no possible reason for binding me, as the narcotic had me completely paralyzed, but he did it nonetheless.

Then he crossed the room to the porcelain tables and busied himself preparing a flask of some lucent and sparkling fluid that seemed to glow with an inner luminosity of its own. The chemical mixture was clear as water, but heavy as oil or mercury, and imbued with glittering motes of incandescent light. With a sinking heart I guessed its nature and my own fate—against which, it is true, I had been warned.

As he prepared the clear sparkling fluid, Sarchimus

spoke to me in a casual tone of voice. He addressed me in an offhand manner whose calm tones belied the inner excitement visible in his face.

"For very long have I sought to perfect this chemical, which is termed the Elixir of Light," he said. "The precise formulation of the recipe has eluded my researches, although I have discovered the principal ingredients. Variation upon variation have I tested, and each has proven a dismal failure. But today, at long last, the being whose mind contains the perfect formula has divulged it to me, and undying life is within my reach."

A prickling of terror went through me. My nakedness tingled with superstitious fear—yet I could not move. There was naught that I could do but lay there helpless and listen to his serene, gloating voice as he prepared the mixture.

"I don't know why I bother to tell you all this," he said, with an unsteady laugh. "I can hardly expect an untutored savage from the wild to understand the secrets of transcendent chemistry! But I am no such fool as to trust my captive; first I will try the mixture on you, and if you derive no ill effects from it, then and then only will I down the Elixir myself. . . ."

He approached me, a beaker of lambent fluid clenched in one slender hand.

Kneeling beside me, he lifted my head and forced the fluid down my throat.

The voluntary muscle-centers of my body were hopelessly paralyzed, but the involuntary centers were unaffected by the drug he had slipped into my brandy. If it had not been so, I would have died, my heartbeat stilling, my lungs failing to expand, permitting me to draw breath. And swallowing, too, is an involuntary action.

The Elixir was tasteless but deathly cold. A numbness spread through me as the fluid was poured down my throat.

I waited for death. Or for the creeping death of petrification.

Sarchimus hung over me, his features pale and taut, glistening with a sheen of perspiration. The agony in his eyes was terrible to see.

Then the numbness that had spread through the center of my being was replaced by a glowing warmth. Vigor surged up within me and the fires of life burned high. A glorious surge of fresh new energy blazed within me—a wondrous new strength went flaming through every fiber of my being!

The expression of agonized suspense in the quicksilver eyes that observed me turned eagerly to a wild joy.

My young chest rose and fell. My thews swelled with the surge of new power. I could feel the strength grow within me; almost I could have thrown off the effects of the narcotic. My sinews trembled and, in the next moment, I was free of the numbness of the drug and fighting the bonds with furious strength. Had they not been fashioned of the incredibly durable transparent metal which was as common on the World of the Green Star as iron is on Earth, I have no doubt I could have burst my chains, for my strength was as the strength of three men in those glorious moments. But they were of the lucent metal I privately thought of as *glassteel*, and all my strength was helpless against them.

Unholy joy transformed the normally impassive visage of the savant to a mask of ecstacy. He snatched up the beaker from its stand with trembling hands and poured the sparkling fluid down his own throat—

Part 3

THE BOOK
OF ZARQA
THE KALOOD

Chapter 11

THE ELIXIR OF LIGHT

Panting, I lay helpless in my bonds. My brown, muscular limbs gleamed with perspiration under the fiery rays of the lamp. I stared through my tousled gold mane at the savant, knowing him victorious. Hoom had spoken wisely; nor had Zarqa overestimated the hazards of the situation. Unknowingly, I had aided in the birth of a tyrant superman whose career, unchecked, would lead him to the dominance of my adopted planet.

The secret of immortality lent him a terrible weapon; in its way, the weapon was more disastrous even than the army of metal automatons now vivified and ranked in wait for his commands. Armed with the superior technology of the Kaloodha, he could whelm and conquer the cities of the Laonese. Armed with the promise of immortality, he could conquer the hearts of the kings and princes of the Green Star, who would sell their sovereignty—and their very souls—for eternal youth.

A grim, ironic smile twisted my lips. I had come a second time to this world, hoping to undo the wrongs I had committed on my first visit. Then, my accidental reincarnation in the person of the heroic Chong had hardened the people of Phaolon in their determination to resist their enemies, the Ardhanese. Then, the princess I loved had fallen into the hands of her deadliest foes, and I had perished in the attempt to set her free—leaving her alone and friendless in the land of her enemies.

Hoping to correct these grievous wrongs, I had flown again in astral form to the World of the Green Star. And now, in this second incarnation as the boy warrior, Karn, I had unwittingly aided the tyrant Sarchimus in vitalizing a mechanical horde of killer machines and in attaining the long-sought secret of personal immortality. Far from improving the situation on this world, I had irreparably worsened it!

I glared through my tousled mane at the exulant face of Sarchimus, to see the effects of the Elixir blaze up within him, transforming him, as it had transformed me, into a superman of tripled vigor.

Instead . . . I saw his features crumble into a mask of horror!

Pale and working, his features fell into sagging folds and he staggered, one bare hand going out to a stone column to steady himself.

And there came, loud in the ringing silence, a most peculiar sound.

The grating of stone against stone.

His eyes fell with unbelieving horror to his own right hand. For it had been the touch of *his bare flesh* against the column that had produced that stony rasp.

I looked at his hand and saw that horror which had transfixed him. For, even as I watched, the mellow ivory tone of his hand paled—whitened—*to the dead, lusterless white of pure chalk.*

Within the space of a single heartbeat his hand was a dead thing of white stone, lifeless as a lump of cold rock.

He staggered about the laboratorium, lurching against the lecterns, overturning the porcelain benches, shrieking in a mindless blasphemy of mad imprecation against the merciless and mocking fates.

Now the petrification attacked his left leg. It became a dead weight which he was forced to drag over the stone pave with a grating sound.

Babbling hoarsely, he staggered and could no longer support the growing weight of his own body. He fell to his knees sobbing, then sprawled face forward on the pave, writhing and foaming at the mouth. His struggles grew fainter as the creeping tide of petrification spread through his limbs; his moaning became fainter.

At last only his mad, despairing eyes lived in a face of dead, carved stone. . . .

The lamps guttered and died, leaving me alone in utter darkness. Throughout the Scarlet Pylon there was only darkness and silence. Naked and helpless, I lay in my chains awaiting death.

But death did not come to me. Some innate factor in

my physical body prevented the sparkling fluid from working its spell of petrification upon my flesh. Could it perhaps be that the lingering traces of *phuol*-venom in my
blood resisted or neutralized the Elixir?

I did not know; I only knew I must live on. Until I died
in the slow agony of thirst and starvation, helpless to free
myself from the chains.

For hours I lay alone in the darkness, listening to the
beating of my own heart in my naked breast. The silence
about me was deafening.

Here I would lie helpless until I starved to death . . . *or
would I?*

For I thought of the horrible *saloogs* that infested the
lowermost tiers of the Scarlet Pylon . . . the monstrous and
unkillable plant-animal hybrids that writhed and squirmed
like monstrous worms through the jungle darkness of the
fungi groves . . . *the hybrid predators held at bay only by
the forces employed by Sarchimus the Wise . . .*

Who now was Sarchimus the Dead.

The lamps had died throughout the tower because they
and the energy sources which fed them were attuned to
the personality of the dead savant who lay behind me
somewhere in the impenetrable darkness, a monstrous
stone thing.

With the instant of the death of Sarchimus, the energy
sources throughout the Pylon had died with him.

Including whatever intangible barriers had held at bay the
gigantic wormlike *saloogs*.

Lying in the black night, I wondered how long it would
be before the mindless hybrids realized the energy barriers
had fallen . . . how long before they writhed up the ascending ramps on their stumpy legs into the upper levels?

Would it be hours—or days—or weeks—before they
crawled to this level of the dead tower?

By then, I knew, hunger and thirst would have enfee-
bled or slain me. When they came slithering to feed upon
my body in the dark I would be helpless to oppose them.

The thought was loathsome.

But I could not drive it from my mind.

And I lay there, naked in the darkness, in the grim
silence, thinking of death.

After a time I slept. Miraculous are the resources of the
human body; even more wondrous are the resources of

the mind. Horror may gibber in its recesses, but exhaustion takes its toll: and a weary man will sleep, however perilous his position.

An unknown interval of time passed.

And suddenly, swiftly, I came awake and lay there motionless in the utter blackness, straining every nerve to hear a repetition of that far, faint sound that had aroused me from my exhausted slumber.

It came again—a faint, stealthy creaking!

A creaking as of the upper ramp which led to this level of the tower.

Often had I noticed that when I trod upon that topmost portion of the ramp, some weakening or flaw within its construction caused a faint creaking.

It came again, that far, slight sound, as of some slow, ponderous weight moving, creeping, ascending the ramp to this level.

In my mind's eye I pictured a huge, swollen, loathsome *saloog* squirming sluggishly over the ramp to this tier of the tower, its bloated and putrescent head lolling blindly in the darkness, as those monstrous and uncanny flower-eyes sought through the darkness the faint warmth of living human flesh—

Of *my* flesh—

I lay, straining every nerve to listen.

All too well did I recall that the portal to this laboratorium was ajar. No barrier opposed itself to whatever hideous abnormality lumbered slowly through the blackness toward where I lay.

Now the sound was within this very room!

I could hear it in the darkness, breathing heavily.

Even now, were I unbound, I could at least still flee, gain the upper levels of the Scarlet Pylon, escape into the giant trees. Or if that way were blocked, at least I could stand and face it with a weapon in my hand. For to go down battling was better than this torment—lying helpless, waiting for the loathsome caress of those thick, cold, fleshy petals against my nakedness, as the slobbering digestive organs began the slow process of devouring its living prey.

The floor creaked.

Something was moving through the darkness toward me.

It did not stand erect, like a man, but slithered and groped on its belly, like a beast.

Stone grated and rasped as the thing fumbled with the dead chalky corpse of Sarchimus.

I held my breath, hoping it would pass me by.

But surely it could hear the drumming of my racing heart in the echoing silence!

A long, agonizing moment crawled slowly by—an eternity of breathless suspense.

Again I heard hoarse breathing.

A hot, panting breath. Very near me now.

The thing was only a few feet away.

Oh, to stand on my two legs and face it with a length of steel in my hands! To face it like a man, and, live or die, to go down fighting! Anything was better than lying here in the dark, waiting for the slow death that crept nearer and ever nearer. . . .

And then I felt it.

Something cold and dry and living was crawling slowly across my thigh and up my belly. . . .

Chapter 12

THE SKY-SLED

And then a silent voice spoke within my brain.

Karn?

Relief sluiced through me like an icy flood, leaving me shaken.

"Zarqa? Can it be. . .?"

The Kalood touched my arm with his dry, leathery hand, felt along it to the wrist-cuff, and began working on the chains that bound me.

Sarchimus is dead, he said mentally. *And with the extinction of his will, those appurtenances tuned to the wavelength of his brain also died or became inactivated. My force-prison suddenly faded and I was free.*

He could not unfasten the chains. I heard him crawling slowly and with difficulty to the petrified corpse of the science magician, searching for the keys. I perceived that he was greatly weakened from his ordeal at the hands of Sarchimus. Long deprivation from the golden mead had taken its toll of his strength. He secured the key and came back to where I lay and began unlocking my bonds.

It is fortunate that the petrification affects only organic matter, he said. *Otherwise this key would be useless.*

I sat up and began massaging my wrists while he fumbled with the chains that bound my feet.

"You gave him the secret formula for the Elixir at last . . . but it was the wrong formula?"

Aye; I could resist him no longer. But I made certain that the Elixir would destroy him when he imbibed it. . . .

"But he tested it on me first," I protested. "Why didn't it turn me to stone, as it did him?"

The one ingredient he did not know acts as a stabilizing factor, inhibiting the petrification, he said. *That ingredient is a chemical derived from the venom of the scorpion*

90

monsters, the phuol. *I knew that Sarchimus would test the mixture on yourself, Karn; but I also knew, or felt fairly certain, that the traces of* phuol-*venom still lingering in your tissues would suffice to neutralize the petrification effect.*

By now he had freed me and I stood without great effort. I peered around in the darkness.

"Zarqa, the force barriers are down. It is only a matter of time before the *saloogs* begin to ascend the ramps into the upper levels. What shall we do?"

We must leave this place. The sky-sled is still operable, its power supplies unaffected by the death of Sarchimus. But, first, I must have sustenance, for I am near the point of death.

Zarqa described the appearance of the mead on which the Kaloodha fed; while he lay exhausted I searched by the light of a small crystal and before long discovered a supply of the honey-like fluid in a cupboard concealed in the wall of the science magician's bedroom. While Zarqa downed a quantity of the golden mead, I made my way to the place where Prince Janchan was imprisoned. The panel was still locked and I could see no way to open it; but the effect of the Elixir of Light was still potent within me, and my strength was that of many men. I seized up a massive bench of polished marble and smashed an entry-hole through the panel, freeing the hapless Phaolonian.

He accompanied me back to the laboratorium where he stopped short and voiced a cry of astonishment at the sight of the strange gaunt, golden-hued aerial creature.

"This is my friend, Zarqa the Kalood," I said. "His people were the ones who built this city, ages ago, and he is the last of his kind on this world. Sarchimus has tortured and starved him to his present condition in order to wrest the secrets of the ancient science of the Kaloodha from him."

The eyes of Janchan were wide with disbelief.

"By the World Above, Karn! We have legends of such beings, but never had I dreamed to meet a creature of myth in the very flesh! Does he understand our language?"

I am unfitted with the organs of vocal speech. Zarqa made his own reply to the question. *The mode of converse we employ is that of mind to mind.*

Janchan swore at the uncanny sensation, as the vibrations of an alien brain sounded among the cells of his own brain.

I know that to your eyes I appear strange and monstrous and malformed, the Winged One said wryly. *But fear me not, Prince Janchan, for consider—you seem to me every bit as strange of form as I must seem to you. Yet are we comrades, sharing imprisonment in common; let us be friends.*

"With all my heart," Janchan swore feelingly. "And forgive me if my reaction to your appearance seemed insulting. Recall, that I knew not of your existence and coming upon you in this manner took me by surprise."

I observed curiously the effects the golden mead were having on poor Zarqa. He had been gaunt to the point of emaciation, his elongated fleshless limbs scarce more than skin and bones, his purple eyes dim and lusterless and enormous in his pinched, hollow-cheeked visage. But the mead was acting as a miraculous restorative. Almost visibly, his attenuated limbs filled out, developing healthy sinews. Brilliance shone in his enormous eyes, and the dull, dry condition of his leathery skin changed rapidly, as his pale golden hide became moist and supple and resilient. The golden mead must be some artificial tonic nutriment, with enormously concentrated food value. In no time, Zarqa was striding about the laboratorium with a swinging stride, his strength nearly normal.

We should be gone from this place within the hour, my friends, said Zarqa. *The hybrid predators which infest the lower levels are not our only danger; Hoom of the Many Eyes will swiftly be apprised of the destruction of his rival, and will come hither from his Opal Spire in all haste, so as to inherit as much of the equipment of Sarchimus as possible.*

"There is sense in what you say," Janchan admitted.

"But Zarqa," I protested, "the Scarlet Pylon is your home; why should you be driven from it, to follow us into the unknown dangers of the forest?"

The Kalood shrugged high bony shoulders.

Never can I be at peace here again, now that the men of your race such as Sarchimus and his kind have made of Sotaspra their domain. Perhaps it is time for me to let the past go, and venture out into the greater world beyond. If so, I can do no better than to make the first of my new purposes in life to be of assistance to you, Karn, and to your friend, to aid you in returning to your homes. There is nothing for me here in Sotaspra, anymore. . . .

We left the laboratorium and went up to the crest of the Scarlet Pylon. The last, level beams of daylight struck through the great canopies of leaves, touching them to burning green-gold, and gilding the corrugated surfaces of the enormous branches. Soon, darkness would come down upon the World of the Green Star. But by then we hoped to be aloft.

We found the sky-sled where Sarchimus had left it, moored to the upper tier. A hangar-like structure protected it from the elements, and the aerial contrivance was powered and ready for flight.

Returning to the apartments below, we rumaged about, Janchan and I, selecting garments. The science magician had stripped me bare and, in the ensuing events, I am afraid I had forgotten my nakedness. Now I searched the closets, finding warriors' gear, a simple leathern tunic, girdle, cloak, and boots. From the armamentarium of the savant, Janchan and I selected weapons. I took a curved scimitar while he chose a slim rapier of glassteel, and we both attached the scabbards of broad-bladed daggers to our trappings. I took the precautions of filling my pocket-pouch with coins from the savant's store. These were of unfamiliar mintage, and cast in the rare, precious metals of the Laonese: a brilliant blue metal they call *jaonce,* a gleaming black metal, heavy as lead, they term *arbium,* and a sparkling transparent metal, clear as crystal, called *kaolon.*

The Laonese metals, incidentally, are extremely rare since the folk of this world never, or very seldom, dare to descend to the floor of their worldwide forest, as those gloomy precincts are the haunt of terrible and legendary monsters. Instead, they distill—as it were—their precious metals from minute traces suspended in the sap of the mountainous trees wherein they dwell. The process is laborious and the metals thus derived, by consequence, far more costly then Terrene gold or silver.

Having filled my pouch, I rejoined Prince Janchan, who had assumed warriors' raiment similar to mine. We bundled up food supplies, dried meats, preserved meats, dried fruits, a jug or two of wine, loaves of a peculiarly nutritive black bread, and several canteens of fresh water.

Then we ascended for the second time to the roof of the tower and began storing these supplies in a storage compartment Janchan found in the rear of the sled. Zarqa had gone below with us, but had vanished about business of his own, and had not yet rejoined us. Janchan fidgeted restlessly, eager to be off.

"Where is your winged friend, Karn? Night is almost upon us, and I would like to be far from the Dead City before darkness makes further flight hazardous."

Even as he spoke, Zarqa came into view carrying a number of objects, which he began stowing away in the side compartments of the flying sled.

"Zarqa, what are these?" I asked.

Merely a few articles salvaged from the possessions of Sarchimus, who no longer has any need for them, he said. *I thought they might prove useful to us on our journey.* Among these was a capacious robe or burnoose woven of synthetic plastic fiber shot through with a web of silvery metallic threads, which Zarqa termed a Weather Cloak. The other articles he named as a vial of Liquid Flâme, a coil of Live Rope similar to that from which the science magician had fashioned my collar, and a floating luminous sphere called a Witchlight.

I have also taken the precaution of bringing along the savant's zoukar, he said, displaying the metal-capped crystal rod with whose captive lightnings Sarchimus had slain the poisonous *phuol. Swords are a primitive kind of weaponry,* he explained, *and my people have always preferred to slay from a distance, wherever possible.*

Janchan surveyed this magical gear dubiously.

"Are we really going to need all these items?" he asked.

Zarqa shrugged, sealing the compartment.

Who can foretell what perils we shall encounter? he asked. *The world is wide and has many dangers. And we shall be but three warriors against many.*

"But you were gone long enough to have ransacked the tower from top to bottom," I said.

Quite right; I had one further mission to accomplish, before we should leave this place forever. One further precaution I took, and that was to render permanently inactive the menacing horde of death-dealing metal automatons Sarchimus had vitalized to further his dreams of empire.

"By the Green Star, I had forgotten all about them!" I swore.

I thought as much. Zarqa smiled. *But it would have been folly to have disposed of Sarchimus, leaving his most dreadful weapons unharmed for Hoom of the Many Eyes to use in his turn. So I have smashed their brain crystals, one by one, and destroyed the breeding vats with a potent acid. Also I released a second tube of Liquid Flame into the science magician's study, saving the only other such for our future needs. The flames will devour all of the notes and formulas and manuscripts of Sarchimus. Without them, or a captive Kalood from whom to torture secrets, Hoom will find it impossible to rediscover the lost sciences, and will thus afford the world no peril such as Sarchimus would have done. And now, I think, we are ready to depart.*

I had thrust into the girdle of my tunic the papers I had received from Hoom. The map was quite simple, orienting the position of the Dead City of Sotaspra in relation to Ardha and Phaolon and a few other cities whose names were unfamiliar to me.

"We have not yet decided where, exactly, we are going," Janchan pointed out. I nodded, saying that I had no desire to return to my own people of the Red Dragon nation, who had staked me out to die before the stings of the scorpion monsters; I then asked Janchan where he wished to go, whether back to the Jewel City of Phaolon, or elsewhere.

He sighed dispiritedly.

"I have sworn a vow never to return to the city of my fathers until I have learned the whereabouts of my princess, Niamh the Fair, and of Kyr Chong, her champion," he said stoutly. "We of the fellowship sworn to rescue her had combed the nearer trees, finding nothing. But from friendly nomads a rumor reached us that Chong and the princess had been taken by a band of forest outlaws to the Secret City of Siona; this was grim news, indeed, for well is it known that Siona the Huntress hates the royal house of Phaolon with a consuming passion, for that the father of the present monarch exiled Siona's father into the wild."

I kept my silence with some difficulty, as my reader can well imagine. I knew, of course, the truth of the story, since I had accompanied the princess to the Secret City on the occasion Janchan mentions; but I could say nothing of

these matters, for that would be to expose myself as the
second incarnation of Chong, and no one would be likely
to believe me, if I told them of it.

However, Janchan was not quite finished.

"Even grimmer is the fact that the hidden base of
Siona's foresters is unknown to we of Phaolon, and a
secret closely guarded by her band. However, it seems
likely to me, after much thought, to assume that Siona's
vengeance would be to sell Niamh to her enemies, the
people of Ardha. Therefore, the best notion that occurs to
me is that I should venture there, hoping to enter the city
in disguise and discover the whereabouts of the princess."

He broke off, smiling at Zarqa and I warmly.

"However, my dear friends, there is no reason why I
should expect you to join me in this quest, which is purely
a matter of importance to we of Phaolon."

I cleared my throat.

"There is no reason why we cannot at least fly you to
the regions of Ardha, since Hoom's map clearly shows the
way. And, once there, we can discuss the matter further."

Since we were agreed, we then entered the sky-sled,
stretched out side by side and prepared for the flight without further ado.

The bottom of the sled was hollowed into depressions
which fitted our bodies, with raised posts for us to clasp
onto. Zarqa lay in the foremost hollow, close up under the
curved, transparent windshield, in order to operate the
controls. These controls were remarkably simple, and I
had long-since memorized the instructions given me by
Hoom for the operation of the sled. But, with Zarqa
among us, there was no need for me to assume the cap-
taincy of the vessel. The sled, after all, had originally been
his.

He activated the energy crystals. A high-pitched humming rose in our ears. The sleek vessel trembled beneath
us, then rose smoothly into the air, riding upon the magnetic currents. In a moment the Scarlet Pylon fell away
beneath us and we were aloft and on our way to Ardha,
the city of Akhmim the Tyrant.

"A high pitched humming rose in our ears."

Chapter 13

THE FLIGHT TO ARDHA

The sky-sled flew with a minimum of sound or vibration. I did not know then, nor have I learned since, anything concerning the actual mode of operation whereby the vehicle navigates the skies. The motor must somehow be attuned to the magnetic currents of the World of the Green Star, but precisely how remains a mystery to me. However, it flew with remarkable speed and the energy crystals which supplied motive force seemed well-nigh inexhaustible. Which reminded me of something.

"Zarqa, what of the golden mead on which your people subsist? Can you find further supplies of the substance elsewhere in the world?"

Fear not for me, Karn, he replied. *The nutritive value of the mead is extraordinary and its effects long-lasting, such is the concentrated nature of the substance. A small flask, taken once in fifty days, will yield me sufficient nourishment. I have brought with me a number of stoppered jars of the mead from my store, and that should satisfy my needs for two years or so. And when this supply has become exhausted, I can prepare more without great difficulty. The mead is a distillation of the honey of the* zzumalak, he continued, naming the giant bees of the forest-world, *saturated with certain mineral salts. The essence of* zzumalak-*honey is not difficult to boil down.*

Just then we were circling the Dead City, in preparation for our flight into the northeast. Janchan voiced an exclamation of amazement, clutched my arm, and pointed behind us. We turned to see an astonishing sight.

The tower of Sarchimus was . . . *dying.*

The Scarlet Pylon had blazed with vivid hue, so different from the dead and lusterless structures around it. We had not noticed before how the fresh and brilliant scarlet had slowly been fading from the remarkable spire. It was now a deepening purple, stained with splotches of putrescent and funereal brown like rotting vegetation. Even as we stared at this singular phenomenon, the tower began to darken into dead black. Soon it differed in no wise from its fellow towers. And the Pylon of Sarchimus was dead.

Thus perishes the fortress which has been my home for a million years, said Zarqa somberly. *Sarchimus must have attuned the organic and living crystals whereof the Pylon was composed to the vibrations of his own brain. When he came to death, the vital forces of the tower itself began to die. . . .*

"Hoom will find little enough to inherit in that black mausoleum," Janchan observed quietly.

I nodded. "It must sadden you to look on at the death of your ancient home," I said comfortingly to Zarqa, who sat hunched and silent, his weird golden visage inscrutable, sadness lingering in his brilliant purple eyes.

The death of my tower is as nothing compared to the death of my city and the extinction of my race, he said finally.

"Surely, you could revitalize the structure, friend Zarqa," suggested Janchan. The gaunt Kalood stretched out his narrow wings in the equivalent of a shrug.

To remain for further centuries in the Dead City is to tempt madness, he said. *I have dwelt too long amid ghosts of the past; to dwell yet further years in yon necropolis, where all my people have died, would be unbearable. Nowhere in the world will I truly find a home, but among new friends such as yourself, Prince Janchan, and my young comrade, Karn, at least I can discover solace for my solitary condition in human companionship.*

He shivered, as if setting aside such doleful recollections.

But, come, my new friends! Let us not dwell upon what is over and past: the future lies ahead of us, thrilling with peril and exploit, bristling with excitement and vigor!

The black towers of the Dead City fell behind us and were swiftly lost from our sight in the gathering shadows. We flew in a meandering path between the Brobdingnagian boles of the sky-tall trees, following the map of Hoom. That flight ended within the hour, as the gathering darkness made it extremely dangerous to continue our

flight during the hours of the night. Ere long, we tethered
the sky-sled to a twig the size of a yacht's mast. The vehicle was capable of hovering motionlessly and weight-
lessly in midair, sustained by the magnetic current alone,
and thus we felt ourselves comparitively safe from the as-
sault of the numerous predators wherewith the wilderness
swarmed. We made a rude meal from red wine, black
bread, preserved meats and fruits, and bedded down for
the night, strapping ourselves into the body-shaped depressions of the sled as a precaution against falling overboard.

The night was warm. The darkness was complete and
total, for seldom did the stars appear visibly in the skies of
this planet, so thick were the silvery mists that enveloped
the World of the Green Star. The roar of hunting beasts,
the hiss of predatory reptiles, the shriek of their startled
prey, soon rendered the impenetrable darkness hideous.
But so great was our fatigue from the cumulative tension
and exertion of the day, that before long we sank into
slumbers so deep that we slept undisturbed till daybreak.

According to the chart I had from Hoom, over three
thousand *farasangs* lay between the Dead City of Sotaspra
and the Yellow City of Ardha.

The *farasang* is a unit of measurement unique to the
Laonese race, and I find it impossible to translate the term
into its nearest Terrene equivalent. This inability to render
farasangs into miles is due largely to the peculiar modes of
travel common on the World of the Green Star.

Consider, if you will, a civilization that does not dwell
upon the continental surface, but miles aloft, in jewel-box
cities built in the branches of colossal trees. Some of these
cities are three or four miles above the surface of the
planet; indeed, I believe the Secret City of Siona's band to
have been at least five miles above ground level.

On the planet of my birth, for humans to have dwelt in
comfort at such mountaintop heights would have been a
physical impossibility, as the atmosphere of the Earth thins
out with height and becomes too rarified and bitterly cold
to sustain human life after a few miles.

But conditions are different on the World of the Green
Star. The position of trees and other vegetation in the bio-
sphere of the Earth is to replace oxygen in the atmosphere. Beasts and birds and men absorb oxygen from the

air and breathe out carbon dioxide. But vegetation inhales carbon dioxide and exhales oxygen.

On Earth the trees grow only to minimal heights, the tallest being the mighty Redwoods of California. But on the World of the Green Star the trees grow four or five miles into the sky, and the size and quantity of their leaves is of comparable enormity. A single tree, on the Green Star World, may bear a dozen times the leaf-surface of a Terrene forest, and produces that same multiple in the quantity of oxygen it releases into the air. Moreover, the oxygen-exhaling leafage is mostly to be found at the greatest heights, among the tops of the trees. On Earth, the thin and rarified stratosphere begins at a comparable height; but on the World of the Green Star, the thickest and most oxygen-rich layer of the atmosphere is found at that height.

Thus it is not really strange that the Laonese cities are built many miles above the surface of the peculiar planet, nor that they encounter no difficulty in breathing at a height comparable to the peak of Mount Everest.

Now, to display what bearing these matters have on the nature of the *farasang* as an untranslatable unit of distance-measurement, consider again what I have already stated as regards the fact that the inhabitants of this world never, or never willingly, at any rate, descend to the continental surface of their planet. Hence they have no conception of a distance-measurment based on geographical interval. On Earth, a mile is the measurement of ground-surface between two positions. But the Laonese *farasang* bears little relationship to such a concept, being a measurement of the *time-interval* between places.

It is, quite simply, the average flying-time between two places. I suppose its relationship to miles could be established by a laborious mathematical calculation, but I have no way of establishing the comparable data. Thus, to say that Sotaspra is three thousand *farasangs* distant from the city of Akhmim the Tyrant is to describe the time required to fly between the cities, figured according to the average flying-velocity of the most common Laonese steed, which is the *zaiph,* the enormous and very beautiful dragonflies the people of this world have tamed and broken to the saddle in lieu of horses.

And lacking any precise method to measure the passage of time on a world devoid of clocks or wrist-watches, I cannot even render the term into its Terrene equivalent in minutes or hours. Based on my own experience, I have concluded to my satisfaction that a *farasang* is approximately forty minutes of flight; but as the sky-sled flew many times more swiftly than any *zaiph*, I cannot even be certain of that. To further complicate matters, the period of daylight on the World of the Green Star seems to me considerably longer than the average of twelve hours wherein we divide a day on Earth. I gather that daylight is at least sixteen hours long on the Green Star World; but here, too, I am unable to be exact. Because of the cloud-cover, and the heavy canopy of foliage, the Laonese cannot with any particular exactitude locate the position of their sunstar. The solar illumination becomes greatly diffused as it passes down through the eternal veil of silvery mists that envelops the planet; it diffuses yet more as it filters through the hundred-mile-wide masses of lucent gold-foil foliage each mountain-tall tree bears up.

I gave up all attempts to calculate the distance we traveled in our flight. The mental system of the Laonese—and of the Kaloodha, as well, it seemed—have something in the nature of a built-in biological clock, whereby they can estimate with considerable accuracy the passing of *farasangs* and of fractions of *farasangs*. The body of Karn of the Red Dragon people doubtless contained such a natural timepiece as well, but I, the intruding spirit, did not know how to "read" it.

At least, I assumed this to be the fact. It must have been so, or else the very employment of the unit of distance would be of no particular use to them, and they would have been forced to invent some mechanical means of measuring time to justify their use of the unit.

It was, at any rate, an interminable succession of diurnal flights and nocturnal moorings before we came into the vicinity of Ardha. During the flight we became much better acquainted, as you might imagine, and there was some slight difficulty about this which I suppose I should have anticipated; but I did not, and at first it annoyed and rather hurt me that my companions seemed to prefer each other's company to mine and very frequently conversed, as it were, "over my head."

It suddenly came to me why this should be so. I was a grown man and had played a leading role in the destruction of Sarchimus and in our escape from the Scarlet Pylon.

But, in the eyes of my companions, of course, I was only a scrawny, half-grown boy!

I have had occasion to mention earlier in this narrative some of the difficulties peculiar to the juvenile body I now inhabited: like any boy, I tended to be shy and inarticulate when among my elders, such as the imposing Sarchimus. Now, because of the adolescent body in which my spirit had found its home, I found myself to a certain degree excluded from the conferences and discussions that occured between Zarqa and Prince Janchan.

Zarqa, of course, had endured for countless millennia, and in his eyes even the prince was a child. But Janchan was at least of mature, responsible age, whereas I was but a wild boy from a primitive tribe. Thus at length, although I came to understand their tendency to talk over my head, discussing matters and making plans without bothering to consult me, treating me at times as if I weren't even there, I could not help being mildly humiliated by the experience. I feel certain that both Zarqa and Janchan would have been shocked and disturbed had they once guessed how this natural tendency of adults to converse with adults hurt and humiliated me. I know that Zarqa held a very special affection for me, as Karn of the Red Dragon had been the first human to sympathize with his unfortunate lot and to make a kindly gesture toward him. And Janchan was unfailingly polite to me, and surely considered us friends and comrades. Nonetheless, it rankled— nor was there anything I could do about it, barring a foolish attempt to explain to them that I was a wandering spirit from a distant planet who had chanced to enter and animate a boy's fresh cadaver.

Before long, the situation changed abruptly.

Our interminable aerial voyage ended quite suddenly one afternoon, as we came into view of a most peculiar structure built along the upper surface of a vast branch which extended from a distant tree-trunk which stood directly in our hurtling path.

Zarqa, as if he had anticipated the moment to a nicety, slowed the flight of the sky-sled, and curved its direction off on a tangent. We circled to a halt behind a screen of heavy foliage.

And I knew that we had at last reached the city of Ardha, the realm of Akhmim the Tyrant, within whose citadel perchance the woman I loved was held a helpless prisoner.

If she yet lived.

Chapter 14

ENTERING THE YELLOW CITY

Neither the gaunt Kalood nor the Phaolonian princeling made any spoken comment on the fact of our arrival—but further proof of the existence of that biological clock that enabled them to measure the passage of *farasangs*—so I cautiously refrained from making my alienage obvious by any such remark myself.

We tethered the weightless sky-sled to the base of a leaf the size of a ship's foresail, and dismounted, crawling out on the narrowing twig as far as was possible, so as to obtain a clear view of our objective.

I have mentioned before that the Laonese are utterly without the fear of heights so common to Earthly men. If such had not been so, doubtless the race would have driven itself into extinction aeons ago, for vertigo, to a civilization which inhabits tree-cities built miles in the air, would be a fatal plague. The body of Karn, of course, was likewise immune to any feeling of giddiness; but my Terrene spirit was not, and I could not help picturing the vertiginous depths of the colossal abyss which extended mile upon mile below my slender and insecure perch.

The twig was about as large around as a full-grown oak tree would have been back on Earth. The bark was corrugated into rough overlapping rings of growth, so, actually, it was not particularly difficult to climb rather far out upon the twig—so long as you did not look down, and avoided thinking of the miles of empty air that yawned beneath your heels.

Zarqa pried the leaves apart with the crystal rod of his *zoukar* . . . and thus I obtained my first good look at Ardha.

Well did I remember the first scene upon which I gazed when first I ventured hither to this planet. I had observed

105

the entourage of Akhmim arriving at the court of Phaolon after a flight from the city of Ardha, to lay a marriage proposal which amounted to nothing less than an ultimatum before the throne of my beloved princess, Niamh the Fair.

Closing my eyes, I can conjure up the image of Akhmim as I saw him in that hour. Tall, cruel-faced, clad in robes of stark, eye-hurting yellow, with a towering miter of sparking black crystals on his head and a jet staff clenched in claw-like fingers.

And now, after all this time, I looked upon the city of my foe.

Not for naught was it called the "Yellow City." For, while the city of Phaolon was built all of multicolored crystals, the city of Akhmim was composed of glittering yellow gems, whose monotony of hue was relieved only by roof-tiles and domes and spire-tips of sparkling black jet.

The city was, of course, without walls—such ramparts having no utility or purpose in a world where the inhabitants travel about by air rather than by land. It simply rose, rank on rank of cube-shaped houses, hexagonal towers, slim, soaring spires, fat swelling domes, beginning at the edge of the huge branch and reaching vast heights toward the center of the branch.

Although unwalled, the city was closely guarded. Minute glittering motes swarmed about the gemmed towers and circled above the extent of the branch. These were Ardhanese warriors, mounted on fighting *zaiphs*.

The problem, Zarqa began without preamble, *is one of entry.*

"Quite right," Janchan murmured. "We cannot just go into the city and demand the person of the princess."

We could, of course, wait for night and fly in, hoping to be unobserved in the darkness.

Janchan shook his head. "Too risky, friend Zarqa! The sky-sled would arouse great curiosity and consternation, for the Ardhanese could never have seen its like."

If that be true, Zarqa mused, *then my own appearance would occasion a similar uproar. For the folk of the Yellow City cannot be expected to have seen a member of the Kaloodha before.*

"Again, quite right, I'm afraid. They would regard you as a creature of legend, a thing out of ancient myth, and your appearance would attract much attention—which, of course, is exactly the thing we want to avoid as much as possible."

I had, by this time, had quite enough of being ignored in these conversations, so at this point I spoke up rather rudely.

"Zarqa can fly us down to the extremity of the branch by night, let us off, and return to a place of concealment, to stay by the sled until we are able to rejoin him," I said boldly. "You and I can then enter the city, asking for a place in the ranks as mercenary warriors."

Zarqa and Janchan exchanged a look of surprise, then glanced at me. Janchan gave voice to a slight, embarrassed laugh.

"Why, that's a very good idea, Karn—a *very* good idea, indeed! However, ah ... I don't think we could pass you off as a wandering sell-sword. Mercenaries are generally grizzled veterans, not fifteen-year-old boys."

I fear I flushed hotly at this; for, of course, I had allowed it to slip my mind again that this body I inhabited was that of a boy, and Janchan was quite right.

"I'm sixteen, not fifteen, and—and, tall for my age!" I said hotly.

"Of course you are, and it really *is* a very good idea," the prince said encouragingly. "But I think it would be better if you stayed here in safety with Zarqa, while I try to enter the city by night and learn something of what is going on...."

"But I don't want to stay here with Zarqa!" I burst out, red in the face with humiliation, "I—I want to go down with you and help find the princess!"

Janchan slid one arm around my shoulder and gave me a comforting pat on the back.

"Of course you do, Karn; I know you do. But, well, I think I have a better chance of going it alone...."

At this point, to make my humiliation complete, kindly old Zarqa chimed in.

I really need your assistance here, Karn my friend! he said heartily. *It will be a job for the both of us, guarding the sky-sled from chance discovery.... I would really hate to try doing it all by myself!*

At this point, I subsided, forcing myself into tight-lipped silence. Not yet had I fully mastered the immature emotions of this body; and, I must admit, I had a horrible suspicion that any moment I was likely to burst into tears!

We returned to the sky-sled and made a brief repast.
Then we began constructing a sort of tent of the immense
golden leaves so as to shelter Zarqa and myself, and also
to hide the vehicle from any chance observation from the
air. It was no particular problem to bend twiglets awry,
tie them securely into their new position with knotted
thongs from our trappings. Soon we had managed a tent-
like affair which would afford us some shelter from rain or
wind, and would shield us from sight. Then we napped, in
order to have our strength fresh for the adventure that
night, and lay, trying to sleep, waiting for the darkness to
come.

Interminable hours later, night came down across the
World of the Green Star and we eased the sky-sled out of
its place of concealment, climbed aboard, and took to the
air again. Zarqa had very carefully memorized by daylight
the route and thus without difficulty navigated virtually
blind to a safe position far down the branch on which the
Yellow City was constructed. Janchan dismounted and
drew a dark, concealing cloak about him. The stalwart
princeling had carefully removed every jeweled badge
from his trappings and, clad in plain, worn leather, with a
basket-hilted rapier of common design, could presumably
pass as a wandering mercenary warrior without question,
at least under cursory inspection.

He had his story carefully prepared. Doubtless by now
word had spread to the farthermost cities of the impending war between Ardha and Phaolon. It would only be
natural for homeless men—rogues, exiles, wandering outlaws—to gather for the looting of Phaolon, which could
not for long hold out against the warrior legions of the
Yellow City. One more foot-weary mercenary would not
be suspected in a city where many hundreds must be now
have come to enlist in the hordes of the conqueror.

He turned to face us, his features hidden in the gloom
beneath a heavy hood. He waved one brawny arm in farewell and I saw the flash of his white teeth as he grinned.

"Farewell for a time, my friends! Zarqa, watch for my
signal and be ready at need! Karn, be a good boy, now,
and help our comrade guard the sled! When next we meet,
it shall be to carry the Princess Niamh to safety. Farewell!"

He turned on his heel and strode lithely away. In a few
moments he had vanished in the gloom.

And he was gone.

And I was utterly miserable.

Zarqa and I made our return flight to the encampment we had chosen without incident. While I doubt not that the chevaliers and guardsmen of Ardha are doubly vigilant by night, no human eye, however keen, can with ease penetrate the unbroken gloom of the nighttime on this cloud-enshrouded planet.

We moored our craft and made a light dinner. I was glum and silent, brooding on my misfortunes. If only I had not taken the body of an adolescent boy, but awaited my chance to enter the form of a full-grown man! As for Zarqa, the kindly old fellow did everything in his power to cheer me up and to get me out of my brooding despondency. I fear I made short reply to his conversational sallies and his attempts to jolly me out of my black gloominess. When we finally decided to call it a day and turn in, I'm sure it was to his relief. A sullen boy who replies only in glum monosyllables makes pretty bad company.

I lay awake, staring at the canopy of golden leaves above my head, for an hour or more.

My position was indescribably difficult to endure. I had envisioned myself, I think quite naturally, as the central figure in an heroic quest to free the woman I loved from the enemies who held her prisoner. But, through the mischance of choosing an immature body, I found myself now cast in the role of subordinate, forced to stand idly by, while another young man, bold and daring and gallant, went venturing off alone into danger, to rescue the heroine of *my* adventure!

Oh, it was intolerable. I tossed and turned, unable to sleep, until at last I settled down and was silent. Poor Zarqa could do little more that try to ignore my mood. The gaunt, golden-winged creature was oddly miscast in the role of one *in loco parentis* to a scrawny teen-ager who wanted to be a hero. I'm sure he was relieved when I finally ceased my restless tossing and composed myself for slumber.

Dawn broke goldenly in the skies of the world of giant trees. Zarqa slept lightly, as do his kind; for a time he lay there, his immense and brilliant purple eyes misted with dreams of vanished splendors and empires of the past. At length he rose swiftly and limberly, performed the cursory

ablutions of a race that imbibe nutriment but lightly, and
even then but once in fifty days, and, leaving me to sleep
undisturbed, turned to busy himself with preparing my
breakfast.

The Green Star climbed higher in the heavens. Shafts of
luminous jade drove down through immense canopies of
golden leafage to illuminate the world of colossal inter-
tangled branches and soaring boles. Immense *zaiphs* with
wings like rigid fans of sparkling mica or sheeted opal
dipped and whirled through the sun-shafts, busily hunting
the smaller insect life which were their prey. No distur-
bance came from the Yellow City in the distance, within
whose winding and labyrinthine ways the gallant young
Prince Janchan went about his secret mission.

The food prepared, Zarqa assembled it on a makeshift
tray made of a chip of scaly, dark-red bark, and set it out
for me. Still there came no sound or movement from my
pallet. At length, deciding I had slept my fill, the golden-
winged being stalked over to the entrance of the tent and
twitched it open. . . .

But I was not in there!

No expression crossed his solemn face as Zarqa looked
swiftly about, discovering that my harness, cloak, boots,
sword-belt, and girdle were also missing.

Chapter 15

THE CRIMSON SIGN

Zarqa was ill-experienced in the ways of adolescent human boys; however, the gaunt Kalood had by this time learned enough of human nature to suspect how deeply wounded I was at not being permitted to accompany Prince Janchan on his adventure. It was obvious to him that I had stolen away from our camp in the darkness of the night, for an adventure of my own.

He knew how sorely Janchan would grieve, if anything happened to me during my ill-advised attempt to enter the city. The Phaolonian princeling would blame himself for having been the inadvertent cause of any peril that befell me.

For a time the tall Kalood stood motionless, thinking and pondering the matter deeply.

At length, he determined that the only thing to do was to go after me. Gathering up a few items of his gear, Zarqa fashioned a rude baldric which he slung over one shoulder. To it he attached the scabbard of the *zoukar*.

Then the sad-eyed Kalood took to the air!

The golden-feathered, yet bat-like wings were fully functional, it seemed. Drumming against the air, they bore him from the surface of the branch into the upper air; then, folding his wings, he fell like a plummet into the depths. Like a golden spear he clove the air, head downward, keen and luminous purple orbs scrutinizing the down-slope of the branchlet as he flashed past it. To the keen eyes of Zarqa the Kalood it was simplicity itself to discern the signs of human passage . . . the place where my bootheel had scuffed away a patch of mold . . . the twiglet I had grasped, breaking under my weight . . . the crumpled bit of bark on which I had rested my full weight.

111

He descended to the stem of the branchlet upon which our camp was built. Here he spread his drumming wings, breaking his fall, searching the upper surface of the limb for further human spoor. Here, of course, I had gone erect and the signs of my passing were fewer.

To a lower limb he dropped, a vertiginous fall into the vast abyss down into whose depths the colossal trunk of the tree dwindled. Here he indeed found signs of my descent, for here I had been forced to employ the length of Live Rope I had taken from the sled's store, and the semi-living glassy coil had bitten deep into spongy bark to support my weight.

And on that lower branch he found a fearful thing.

Blood.

For here a battle had been fought. Zarqa's keen eyes clearly read the signs of a struggle—the scuffed and broken bark which I had disturbed underfoot as I fought against a mysterious adversary whose identity Zarqa could not conjecture—a torn scrap of my cloak, still caught on a snag—and blood, blood all over, dripping in rivulets of gore between the corrugations of the bark-rings.

Zarqa stooped over the bloodstain, examining the crimson sign intently.

Was it my blood—or the blood of my enemy?

There was simply no way for him to tell the answer to that question.

His gaunt face grim with despair, the loyal Kalood launched himself into space again; airborne, great wings plying the breeze, the million-year-old creature began to search for any sign of me, living or dead.

But after that terrible crimson sign there was ... nothing!

The predators who rule the wilderness of the giant trees are many and fearsome.

There are wild *zaiphs*, which, although they seldom turn upon men, have no compunctions against devouring their sometime masters and can be the deadliest of adversaries.

More to be dreaded are the colossal white-furred spiders, whose webs are built between the boles of the enormous trees themselves, and some of which stretch across a greater distance than the Golden Gate Bridge on my native planet.

The most feared of all, perhaps, are the rapacious and

reptilian *ythids;* it would have been an irony of fate had Karn the Hunter fallen to their merciless charge, for his nation, the Red Dragon tribe, takes the *ythid* as its tribal emblem.

I could, of course, have simply slipped and fallen into the abyss; this does happen to the Laonese, although not very frequently, since they have a superb head for heights and are as surefooted as mountain goats. But the signs of my struggle, and in particular that huge and ominous blotch of blood, seemed to indicate that I had been attacked by some predator, with whom I had fought.

Whether in that struggle I had been the conqueror or the conquered, Zarqa did not know. But he did not despair; it is not the nature of his kind to yield to destiny, but to fight on until even the last chance was lost.

Towards night he gave over the search for a time, at least, for even his preterhuman constitution required rest.

But he had come by now a very long way from our encampment. To return to it seemed futile, for to continue the quest on the following morning would first require his retracing his flight all the way to where he now crouched resting on a twiglet.

And so Zarqa simply decided to stay here for the night. He would require no further sustenance for many weeks, and his gaunt and leathery hide needed no covering against the night's chill. So he simply roosted there on the twiglet, his head tucked under one great wing, sleeping as soundly as the enormous bat he resembled.

With dawn he awoke, stretched, relieved him, drank a little clear cold water from a pool of dew cupped in an upturned leaf, and flew on about his quest. It was his intention to search the entire tree in a careful and methodical fashion. He assumed there was no means by which I could have crossed to the other tree, on whose branch the Yellow City was built; therefore, his search was, for the present, confined to the tree in which he had spent the night.

His search was terminated brutally and swiftly.

A piercing pain stabbed through him suddenly as he was in mid-flight.

He turned to see a terrible black arrow had pierced the drumhead-taut membrane of his right wing.

Already he was losing momentum as air leaked through

the torn membrane; the wound gaped wider—it was being torn open by the pressure of the wind. He curved in his flight to settle on the nearest branch.

But before he could land, a second black arrow flashed toward him and caught him in the wing-joint itself.

Bright agony lanced along his nerves. His senses dimmed as the entire wing went numb.

Then he tumbled from the air, his injured wing unable to bear him up, and fell like a dead weight. . . .

When he regained consciousness, Zarqa found himself stretched out on a branch surrounded by human beings. They were rough-looking men, with hard faces and vicious eyes, clad in the bright yellow japons and black cloaklets of the Ardhanese. They carried slim glassteel swords, hooked pikes, knobbed maces of black crystal, and each bore an enormous black bow.

They were arguing among themselves as Zarqa returned to consciousness and did not at first notice that he was awake. He seized that brief opportunity to ascertain the extent of his injuries. He had broken his left arm when he fell from the sky, as he learned from the stabbing pain that went through him when he tried to move it. His right wing was disabled, perhaps permanently, although so numb was the wing that he could not tell whether the black arrow had crippled the joint or merely passed through the flesh of it. He still wore his baldric, although the *zoukar* and its sheath had been unclipped, as the crystal rod resembled some kind of weapon.

Since he was unable to fly with his crippled wing, and could not very easily climb because of his broken arm, there seemed to be very little chance of making an escape. So, with the vast and patient pessimism of his kind, Zarqa simply awaited the next turn of events.

He listened to what the men who stood about were saying, hoping to gain some knowledge of their purpose toward him. A burly rogue with unshaven jowls was loudly cursing at the moment.

"By the Fangs of Balkh, I say let's kill the thing here and be about our business! Even if it's an *amphashand* or no, we'd no intent to hurt it, so what's the pity? Claws of Aozond, mates, we thought it was a golden moth—"

." '*We?*' What d'you mean?" growled one of the others, a wizened little man with a twisted back. " 'Twas *you*, and you alone, cut down the blessed *amphashand* with your black arrow, Gulquond—none of *our* doing!"

The others growled nervous assent at this, and the burly rogue the wizened little man had addressed as Gulquond flinched and paled visibly at the accusation. He licked his lips and his piggish little eyes flickered around as if desperately searching for a way out of the trap into which he had fallen.

Zarqa knew little enough about the religious beliefs of the human beings who shared this planet with him, but he understood that they considered the unknown region above the cloud banks to be the home of whatever various gods and genii and elementals and avatars they worshiped. And, as it chanced, he understood enough of their beliefs to know that the winged servants of these many godlike beings were called *amphashands*. . . .

The members of the Ardhanese hunting party thought they had shot down *an angel!* If the situation had not been so dangerous, it would almost have been comical.

The main tenor of Gulquond's argument was that the gaunt winged creature he had shot down by accident was no *amphashand* but merely a winged monster of some unknown kind, who must have descended to the tree-level from the unknown heights of the sky. He counseled they should cut its throat, tip it over the branch into the abyss, and be on their way.

An older man, with grizzled beard and streaks of silver in his fine, floating hair, thought otherwise. He kept turning over and over thoughtfully in his hands the *zoukar* he had taken from Zarqa's baldric. Within the crystal tube a shaft of blue-white lightning writhed and snapped virulently.

"Monster the thing may be, but it goes armed like a creature from The World Above," he said gruffly. "Look here, Gulquond, and quit your sniveling . . . what monster carries around a *bolt o' lightning* instead of a sword?"

The other rogues crowded near to stare at the writhing thing with superstitious awe. Fear was clearly written on their faces.

"No," said the older man, whose name Zarqa learned was Kalkar. "This is too important a matter for us to decide; I say let's carry the monster or whatever it is before Arjala for judgment and disposal . . . creature's got a busted arm, besides that broken wing . . . let's make a stretcher from a couple of tents and poles, and carry it down real careful . . . if it dies before we get it to Arjala, she'll have our hides, I warrant!"

They had, none of them, addressed a single word to Zarqa, although the older man, their leader, soon realized he was now conscious again. Perhaps they were afraid to speak to the winged creature armed with a lightning bolt, who might be either a horrible flying monster from the upper sky or a blessed messenger of the gods; more likely, thought Zarqa with grim humor, they did not think so inhuman a creature capable of speech. At any rate, while they bound him, Zarqa kept his silence. The touch of an alien mind might be too shocking an experience for men already possessed with superstitious awe.

They handled him with gingerly care, removing the black arrow from the joint of his wing, and placing his broken arm in a rude sling which they bound against his breast so that it would not be jolted, causing him pain in travel. Then they put him in the hastily-improvised stretcher, bound him in with a couple of straps, and began making their way down the limb. Zarqa fainted twice during the passage, and, as it happened, was unconscious at the end of the journey.

It occurred to him that he was rather ineffectual. In attempting to rescue the boy Karn, he had himself become a captive.

And so they bore Zarqa the Kalood down to the limb upon which their *zaiphs* were tethered and bundled him into a wain drawn by a team of enormous moths called *dhua*. The wain had obviously been intended to carry the bodies of the beasts they had hoped to take in their hunt.

Instead, they had taken a far stranger and rarer prey.

The hunters mounted; their dragonfly steeds arose on thrumming fans of sparkling opal. They left the branch one by one and soared between the trees and came circling down in the inner precincts of Ardha. And the heart of Zarqa sank within him as he discerned the nature of the enormous building in whose courtyard they landed.

It was the Temple of the Gods, and the Arjala of whom the hunters had spoken must be the priestess or prophetess of the Temple. And who in all Ardha should know better than she that he was no *amphashand?*

Part 4

THE BOOK
OF JANCHAN
OF PHAOLON

Chapter 16

SWORDS IN THE NIGHT

In essence, the plan of Prince Janchan was simplicity itself. That is to say, he had no plan at all.

Karn's notion of attempting to enlist as a wandering mercenary was just the sort of immature, romantic notion an impulsive youngster would dream up. Thus, of course, he had given it no thought at all. All he had in mind to do, at this stage of the game, was simply to get in the city and wander about, picking up what information he could, holding himself in readiness to follow any direction that looked promising.

Entering the city was no problem at all.

The tree-cities of the Laonese, as I have said, lack walls for obvious reasons. The edges of Ardha were the slums, a huddle of sheds and hovels crouching against warehouses and barracks as if for protection. It proved not difficult for Janchan to insinuate a path through these dilapidated lean-tos. He emerged at length into the city itself, unseen or at least unnoticed, an ordinary figure in his dark woolen cloak with the hood shielding his visage, a figure garbed in the plain leathern trappings of a swordsman. Every noble house retains its own entourage of guardsmen recruited from landless or untitled fighting-men, and Janchan could pass for any one of a thousand such, unless he was asked to show the badge of his allegiance. Had any noted him as he strode swiftly and quietly down the street they would have thought him merely a guardsman out for a night of pleasure in the wineshops and alehouses of the city. In point of fact, Janchan made his way directly to just such an establishment, as soon as he ascertained which portion of the city he had entered.

Having found a street lined with such accommodations, he picked the largest, reasoning that where wine flows freely tongues become loosened and one who keeps his wits about him, his ears open, and the wine cup from his lips, may pick up a quantity of useful information. Since his purse was filled with coins he chose the largest and most luxurious of the lot.

It was an establishment rather unique to the Laonese, called a pleasure garden. Pleasure gardens combine all the most conspicuous conveniences of a wineshop and a house of women, with extensive facilities for gambling and sport on the side. The pleasure garden he chose was called the Garden of Nocturnal Delights, and he entered by an unobtrusive side entrance, inserting a small coin in something remarkably like a Terrene turnstile, and went through, finding himself among miniature flowering trees and winding artificial streamlets, with fountains tinkling somewhere and soft laughter coming from the shadows of the bushes. Colored paper lanterns were strung between the boughs and from the distant gambling hall he could hear singing and laughter and the sound of musical instruments.

He was making his way through the gardens toward the gaming house which rose in the center of the grove of fragrant trees, when a low, tinkling laugh sounded behind him. He turned swiftly, one hand going to his sword, to look into the amused eyes of a young woman. She was, he perceived, remarkably attractive, her lissome form clothed in light draperies, with quantities of small bells woven in her silvery hair.

"Did you think me an Assassin, swordsman?" She laughed at his discomfiture. "I assure you that such is not the case. Would you like to buy me a cup of wine?"

Janchan was about to decline her offer of companionship, then changed his mind on the spur of the moment: to do so might make him conspicuous.

He forced a smile. "Thank you, I would be delighted." The girl took his arm, led him to a bench beneath a flowering tree and rang a bell, summoning a servitor, who poured them two goblets of a highly spiced beverage. Janchan could tell the wine had been spiced to conceal the fact that it was watered down. He toasted his companion and drank lightly.

"My name is Kaola." The girl smiled. "And the price of my company is one *gambok* for the evening." Janchan gave his own name and handed her the coin, which she pocketed—although he could have sworn her revealing garments contained no hiding place for so much as a single coin. Sharing the wine, they chatted lightly, and Janchan gave out that he was an unattached warrior who hoped to take service in the entourage of some noble lord here in Ardha, having but recently come hither from another city named Kamadhong. Kaola listened with interest and made intelligent comments; he deduced that the girl was a professional companion, and, as such, must have been trained from childhood. Girls of this class are called *thiogiana* and are trained to be graceful, witty, accommodating, and charming, skilled in the arts of conversation. They are not exactly prostitutes; their role in Laonese life is more like that of the hetaerae of ancient Greece. She was attractive enough, he thought, with silky, glittering hair and immense and brilliant amber eyes; he began to relax, tossing back the hood of his cloak.

"You should find no difficulty in procuring employment here," the girl advised him, "for the princes of Ardha strive to outdo one another in the size and impressiveness of their entourages. The city is divided into two groups of rival factions, you will find. One group sides with the Royal Akhmim, our hereditary ruler, while the other, which is called the Temple Faction, gives their allegiance to Holy Arjala."

"Who is this Arjala?" he asked idly.

"The incarnation of the Goddess and the intended bride of Royal Akhmim," the girl replied. "Akhmim has himself caused the factional divisions by breaking with tradition; our rulers customarily wed the supreme avatar of the Goddess in each generation, but the Tyrant has spurned his intended for another."

"Something of this has already come to my ears," he said. "I have heard that Akhmim desires to wed with the regnant Princess of Phaolon, hoping thus to extend his kingdom. . . ."

Kaola shrugged. "I fear the Great Prince has developed ambitions of empire." She laughed. "Indeed, he presented his suit to the Phaolonian court and, when rebuffed, mounted an invasion. Ere the attack could be launched, however, the Princess of Phaolon fell into the hands of forest outlaws who sold her to the envoys of Akhmim. He would thereupon have forced his suit upon her, had not Holy Arjala forestalled him by abducting the captive princess, thus bringing about a stalemate."

Janchan listened to this news with a careful pretense of casual interest; actually, his heart was beating with excitement. The girl expanded on her information, seeing his interest.

"Arjala, as titular Goddess, can do as she pleases. She sent the Temple Guard into the palace, carried the princess off under pretense of offering her sanctuary in the Temple; she holds her captive there, well-treated, I am told, while attempting to force Akhmim to a showdown. Meanwhile, her agents have divided the city into rival factions, the one side claiming the Tyrant's wedding will extend the power of Ardha to imperial glory, the other warning that his break with tradition will anger the Gods. It is all very amusing; Akhmim seethes with rage, but cannot openly move against the Goddess Incarnate; the Goddess loathes Akhmim, but must wed him in order to attain the queenly power she desires. Neither side gains supremacy in this stalemate, and the only winner is the city of Phaolon itself, which would else have fallen to our siege long-since."

"A remarkably complicated situation," Janchan said indifferently. "How long can this stalemate endure?"

The girl shrugged bare shoulders. "Not long, I venture. Holy Arjala has but recently allied herself with the Assassins' Guild, which is very powerful in this city. It is rumored that for this alliance she promised Gurjan Tor, the chief of the Assassins, the full revenues of the Temple for one year. Obviously, the Goddess hopes to tip the balance of power through a judicious series of murders, robbing the Royal Faction of a few of its most important adherents ... more wine?"

Janchan nodded and held out his goblet. But at that very instant an inarticulate cry reached his ears from beyond the hedges. And instant later he heard the scuff of sandals upon the walks strewn with wood chips, and the familiar clash of sword against sword.

He sprang to his feet, overturning the tray of drinkables. Snatching out his sword and tossing back his cloak so that it should not encumber his arms, he forced his way through the hedge and found himself looking upon a tense scene.

A burly, heavy-faced warrior in a long japon of yellow silk stood with his back against a tree-trunk. Blood leaked from a wound in his right shoulder and his right arm dangled limp and useless. In his left he clenched a stout sword with which he held at bay three masked men in black who were attempting to come at him from three sides at once.

The quarrel was none of Janchan's business, of course. But the prince could hardly stand by and watch what amounted to murder in cold blood. His innate sense of chivalry demanded that he lend his sword to the defense of the wounded and outnumbered man. So, without pausing for a moment to weigh any cautious considerations, he sprang from the hedge and engaged the blade of the nearer black-garbed swordsman.

The heavy-set man in yellow cast him a surprised glance, then smiled grimly.

"Welcome, friend!" he boomed heartily. "Feel free to enjoy yourself, if you feel in need of a bit of exercise—it does wonders for the appetite, they say."

Janchan laughed, his agile point scratching his opponent on one black-clad shoulder. "I was wondering if this was a private argument, or if anyone might join in; your words assure me of my welcome."

The other chuckled. But then their three assailants redoubled their efforts and neither Janchan nor the injured man had breath enough for further jests. The black-masked men fought in complete silence, and were experienced swordsmen of considerably skill. But Janchan's unexpected entry into the ambush had taken them by surprise, and the Phaolonian princeling was lucky enough to disarm his opponent at the onset, and to drive his point through the sword-arm of the second, while the injured man readily dispatched the third, without great difficulty.

Having enough of the combat, the three melted into the shadows and took to their heels. Janchan turned to see to the injured man, who was breathing heavily and evidently suffering considerable pain from his shoulder-wound.

"I appreciate your assistance, my friend," the other grunted. Before Janchan could reply, two men in yellow tunics came pelting up the garden walks to assist their comrade. Bundling him in a heavy cloak they led him into the gaming house, but before this he wrung Janchan's hand in thanks and pressed a small crystal token upon him.

"From your unadorned trappings, I perceive your loyalties to be unengaged. Meet me tomorrow at the morning meal, and I will requite your gracious assistance in any manner I may."

. They assisted their wounded comrade away, leaving Janchan with a bemused smile. He had made a friend, obviously; but he had no idea who he might be. Shrugging, he turned to reenter the alcove where Kaola awaited him.

"Marvelous!" The girl laughed, eyes sparkling. "You have the knack for winning influential friends, swordsman. Or is it possible you do not know that the man you rescued from the three Assassins was Unggor, the captain of Akhmim's personal guard?"

Chapter 17

THE MESSENGER OF HEAVEN

Janchan spent that night in a public house, where for a coin of small value he rented a cubicle and a sleeping pallet. With dawn he hurried to the palace quarter and sought the guard barracks, where the crystal token Unggor had given him gained him quick entry to the captain himself, whom he found propped on pillows, his burly shoulder swathed in bandages.

Unggor's heavy face lightened at the sight of him, and he hailed him with loud welcome, ordering breakfast for the two of them and bidding Janchan be seated.

"My aides bore me away to safety too swiftly last night for me to thank you adequately for coming to my assistance as you did; permit me, then, to offer you my thanks now."

"You need say nothing." Janchan smiled. "I have always thought three against one to be rather unfair odds. How is your wound?"

Unggor shrugged, then winced at the pain. "A trifle, although it will be days before I can use my sword-arm with ease." Gesturing to the heavily-laden tray a subordinate set on a low taboret between them, he invited Janchan to help himself, which the princeling did without ceremony, being famished. Smoked fish and spiced meat and cheese were a Spartan repast, but appetite made a sauce that rendered the simplest meal delicious, he found. While they ate, they looked each other over candidly.

Unggor was a grizzled veteran in his middle years, heavy-set and burly-shouldered, with keen dark eyes and a massive jaw marked with an old knife-wound. His demeanor was gruff and curt, but he was obviously a man who repays his debts willingly.

"In what way can I requite your kindness in helping to

fight off the Assassins?" he inquired. Janchan shrugged and laughed.

"You can offer me employment, to be frank. I have been two days here in Ardha and my purse is somewhat deflated."

"Nothing would please me more," Unggor said. "You are a personable young man and an adroit hand with a blade. You seem intelligent and well-spoken, and I suspect a man of breeding. Where have you served before coming to Ardha, and in what capacity?"

"Kamadhong, where I was a lieutenant in the monarch's guard," Janchan said.

"And why did you leave so favored a position?"

Janchan grinned ruefully. "The colonel of the guard had a mistress who was wont to cast lingering glances on young lieutenants who were not exactly ugly. I fear she cast one glance too many on this lieutenant, for my commission was canceled rather abruptly and it was intimated to me that Kamadhong could do without my presence. I came hither, hoping to repair my fortunes."

Unggor was watching him thoughtfully.

"Why to Ardha, rather than Phaolon, which would have been a briefer journey for you to undertake?" he inquired keenly.

"Briefer, yes, but perhaps costly in the long run. For rumor had it among the guardsmen of Kamadhong that the Jewel City would ere long suffer siege or invasion at the hands of the Ardhanese."

"All the easier, then, to procure employment," Unggor said shrewdly. "A city in danger of war pays well for swordsmen."

Janchan was sweating under his garments, but maintained a frank and casual manner. The captain of the King's Guard was no fool, and mere gratitude would not prove sufficient to allay his suspicions. It might have occurred to him that the assassination attempt had been a ruse, designed to enable an agent of his enemy to procure a position within the palace.

Janchan met his gaze openly. "I prefer to enlist on the winning side," he said. "I am chivalrous enough to lend my sword to an unequal struggle, but heroism has its limits and in war I prefer to stand with the victor."

Unggor burst out laughing, and slapped his knee with his good hand.

"An honest answer, and one I understand." He grinned. 'Well, swordsman, unfortunately the Royal Guard is reserved to those of noble Ardhanese birth; but I am free to choose my own personal entourage, and you may join my retinue if you desire. Clothing and quarters are paid for by our royal master, and your salary is ten *gampoks* the quarter. What say you to this?"

"A hungry man is a willing worker," Janchan observed. "My Captain, I am yours to command!"

Janchan entered the royal service without further ado and was assigned quarters in the guard barracks near the palace enclosure that same morning. Unggor's chief lieutenant, a tall, dour-faced warrior call Ultho, saw that he was equipped with full kit and mess tokens and bedding, and left him to his own devices until the noon muster. Janchan had a small cubicle to himself in the central hall of the barracks, and its furnishings consisted of a woven-reed pallet and a small taboret, with a wall cupboard for his gear. This gear consisted of a gilt cuirass and plumed helm, a long surcoat of yellow silk with the black emblazonry of Akhmim on its breast, and a change of tunics, likewise yellow and black. When he was on guard mount or parade duty, he would draw from the armory buckler, spear, and war boots.

The personal entourage of the captain of the Royal Guard was a handpicked squad of about a dozen warriors, drawn from all levels of Ardhanese society, the prime requisite of their posiiton being weapons expertise, war experience, and their personal loyalty to their chief. Janchan found this refreshingly informal after the tight aristocratic caste system familiar to him from his days in Phaolon; the Jewel City had a rigid aristocracy in which name and breeding counted for everything, and one's station in society was a matter of birth rather than excellence. There were certain elements to the Ardhanese civilization he found preferable to the static culture of Phaolon, he was forced to admit.

His duties were neither arduous nor complicated. Every third day he stood night-guard before the apartments of his captain, and was required to accompany Unggor when he went abroad in the city or attended the court, to shield him against the ever-present danger of assassination. Thus Janchan had several opportunities to observe at close hand

the Tyrant of Ardha, whom he had never seen. This
Akhmim, who had been such a fanatic enemy of the
Phaolonians, was a tall, gaunt man with cold eyes and a
vicious mouth, with a sharp tongue and suspicious manner.
He chafed visibly at the stalemate into which the wiles of
Arjala had placed him, and Janchan accompanied Unggor
to many palace councils devoted to plans for the disrup-
tion of the Temple Faction.

This Arjala, he learned, was hereditary archpriestess of
the Temple, and was considered the avatar or reincarnation of the Goddess, and had been from birth. The Goddess in question was rarely worshiped in Janchan's home-
land, Phaolon, and he was thus unfamiliar with her cult.
She was a nameless divinity, like most of the higher Gods
of the Laonese, who consider that to know the True
Name of any being gives one a certain degree of control
over that entity. Hence most personal names used by the
people of the Green Star World are in the nature of pseu-
donyms, their True Names being closely-guarded secrets.
To know the True Name of a God would be an impiety of
the highest degree, of course.

To be the Goddess Incarnate, and thus supreme head of
the Ardhanese religion, would be power enough to suit the
most ambitious appetite, Janchan thought. But Arjala
would not be satisfied until her temporal authority
matched her spiritual power, and the queenship of Ardha
was her dearest desire. At present, she and Akhmim were
evenly matched in their power struggle; but before many
days had passed, this balance of power was to change in a
surprising manner. . . .

The Flower Boat Festival drew near, and the palace
guardsmen were issued special adornments for the occasion. This event celebrated the birth of the Divine Dynasty
which ruled both The World Above and The World Below; the Festival consisted of processions, feasts, regattas,
and religious rituals. As Akhmim had very special reasons
for wanting to flaunt the royal authority before the rival
factions, he spared no expense to insure that his procession
should outshine all others, especially that to be led by
Holy Arjala.

The treasury was opened, and the Royal Guards were
outfitted with stunning accouterments: each was to wear a
cuirass of solid *xorons,* which are sparkling yellow crystals.

Their helms were to be fashioned entirely of the precious black metal the Laonese call *arbium,* and they were to wear cloaks of woven metal adorned with rows of alternately yellow and black sequins of precious metal. The cumulative effect should be stunning: each guardsman would be wearing the equivalent of the wealth of a sub-province. As for Ákhmim, the monarch himself would ride in the procession in a shell-like chariot drawn by matched *dhua* and carved from pure sparkling *kaolon.* Janchan's comrades felt certain the processions of their rivals would make a poor showing against so ostentatious a display; in particular, the Temple procession was expected to suffer by comparison.

Matters turned out otherwise, though, as they often do.

The day of the Festival dawned bright and clear. Trumpets rang from spire and tower; banners unrolled on the breeze their rich heraldic imagery; children strewed the streets of Ardha with blossoms. Glittering in the dazzle of sunlight, the Royal procession rolled from the palace enclosure and entered the major avenue of the city, which was known as the Ptolian Way.

At the same moment the gates of the Temple were thrust ajar and Holy Arjala rode forth in a mighty chariot covered with sparkling jewels. She was a stunningly handsome woman, her white-gold mane floating behind her like a silken banner, her breasts cupped in hollowed, enormous rubies. She bore the attributes of the Goddess, a jewel-studded Wheel and a stylized Thunderbolt of precious azure *jaonce.* In her train walked a hundred virgins, a hundred priests, and her personal guard of a hundred warriors, robed in scintillant mail. Vast bowls of incense were borne to either side of the procession, their fumy vapors fragrant on the fresh morning air.

Before the chariot of Arjala walked her archpriest and pontiff, a towering man of impressive mien and stentorian voice.

Both processions wound their way slowly from opposite sides of Ardha toward the great Forum of the Ptolian Kings at the heart of the metropolis. The procession of Akhmim amazed the populace with its display of costly gems and metals; the procession of Arjala, however, struck awe and wonder into its heart, but for an entirely different reason. They met at the center of the enormous stone plaza, and a gasp of amazement went up from the

Royal Faction when they beheld what rode with Arjala in her jewel-studded chariot. Silence fell over the immense throng. Akhmim paled and bit his lip with vexation.

Into the silence the deep voice of Arjala's pontiff boomed out a proclamation, timed for maximum effect.

"Behold, O King of Ardha! Behold, O our beloved and faithful subjects! The Lords of The World Above have honored the Holy Goddess Arjala above all mortals and the hour of Her divine apotheosis is come! The Divine Ones now command that the ceremonial nuptials of King and Goddess be celebrated without delay ... *and in token of this, behold the blessed messenger of the Gods who hath descended to The World Below to bear the commandment!*"

There could be no doubt even in the minds of Akhmim's most loyal faction, for there, bearing the sacred torch that was his emblem, a winged and terrible *amphashand* rode behind Arjala.

And only Janchan knew him for Zarqa the Kalood!

Chapter 18

A DANGEROUS MISSION

Arjala had stage-managed her apotheosis with a superb sense of drama. When her huntsmen brought to her the captive Kalood, she knew at once what the creature was, for she had read the ancient legends of his race, and, although she had always considered the Winged Men to be merely creatures of myth, she was clever enough to revise her opinions when evidence appeared to the contrary.

The Kalood was enough like the *amphashands* her religion taught were the blessed messengers of the Gods to pass for one with a bit of makeup. In fact, it now seemed likely the *amphashands* of legend were based on early Laonese memories of the last surviving Kaloodha. For the sacred scriptures described these heavenly messengers as winged men in golden armor, taller and nobler than mortal men, and with imposing beards and flowing manes. The golden armor was evidently mistaken for the leathery, pale-gold hide of the naked Kaloodha, and the beards must be purely the result of human imagination, for Zarqa's folk, like himself, were completely hairless. With the great Flower Boat Festival only twelve days away, the Goddess instantly perceived what a dramatic coup it would be to ride in procession with a heavenly messenger accompanying her. She instantly began spouting commands. Her physicians were to work night and day to heal the injuries Zarqa had suffered from her huntsmen, and strict secrecy was imposed on the entire Temple staff, who were sternly warned not to utter a word concerning this gift that had come down from the skies, on peril of their lives. As they well knew the fiery temper of their divine mistress, and had more than once felt the lash of her wrath, they complied. Thus, no slightest hint of the coming revelation reached the ears of Akhmim's spies.

131

The day of Festival dragged through somehow. The regatta of flower-decorated boats, the aerial races of *zaiph*-drawn chariots, the ceremonial games and dances. And through them all, Akhmim seethed and simmered, seated in the high cupola of honor, with the smug, smiling Arjala at his side. He was forced to defer to her at every turn, and his humiliation was almost more than he could bear, as were the gloating glances she cast at him from time to time, and the demure but pointed remarks she made concerning their coming nuptials. There was absolutely nothing he could do except nod and smile; but once the Festival was over and he had returned to the palace, he paced his council chamber like a raging beast, summoning his councillors, among whom came Unggor, with Janchan in his train.

Plan after plan was offered, discussed, and ultimately rejected. Akhmim was not above having Arjala poisoned or done away with in some similar manner; then it was pointed out to him that she had already purchased the allegiance of the powerful Assassins' Guild, and there was no one else to do the deed but one of the Assassins.

One of the royal councillors, however, had a plan that merited some thought. This was a plump, placid, Buddha-like little man, the Lord Onqqua, who served as chamberlain to the Tyrant.

"Sire, if it is impossible to do away with Arjala herself, it has yet to be demonstrated impossible to do away with her *amphashand*," he purred in a buttery voice.

Akhmim shot him a keen glance from cold, slitted eyes.

"Go on," he grated in a harsh voice. The fat little chamberlain rubbed his jeweled fingers together judiciously.

"I will warrant that few of us are so credulous as to entertain any belief that this peculiar winged creature is actually an *amphashand*. Whatever it may be, it is a living monster, doubtless some inhabitant of the upper skies, either sold to Arjala or captured by her. The creature has the light of intelligence in its eyes; I studied it carefully, during the pontiff's oration. But whether it is merely a manlike and winged beast or some species of intelligent being, it doubtless desires its freedom. Well, I submit that we should set it free."

"What good would come of that?" snapped Akhmim peevishly.

The chamberlain spread his hands with a benign smile.

"Why, the poor creature would fly away home ... leaving Arjala without an *amphashand* to support, by its very existence, her claim to apotheosis. Helpless to display the winged monster before the people, to further dazzle and impress them, it becomes her word against ours—her interpretation of the message, I should say. For who is to say that Arjala had correctly understood the commandment borne to her by the blessed messenger of The World Above?"

"Well, who is to say she hasn't?" Akhmim snarled.

"We are, Sire; or, rather, *you* are. For we can give it out that on the very night of the great Festival, the *amphashand* left the quarters of Arjala and flew into your own chambers, with the word that in her haste and impatience the Holy Arjala perverted or misinterpreted or failed to fully understand the essential meaning of the message the blessed one bore to her from the Gods. The meaning of her apotheosis is that the Gods desire to raise her at once among them; that is, Sire, that she must die. . . ."

A gleam came into the eyes of Akhmim.

"Not bad, Onqqua ... really, not bad at all ... but will anyone swallow it?"

The Buddha-like little man smiled gently.

"Everyone will, Sire—since Arjala will not be able to *produce* the winged messenger in person and thus refute your claim that he left her to visit you."

Akhmim rubbed his long chin and smiled a reluctant smile.

"I perceive considerable merit in your plan, Onqqua; yes, there is much to it. However, with the Assassins pledged to the support of the Temple, who is to steal into the Temple precincts and release the flying monster?"

"Preferably, someone unknown to the Temple priests: any common citizen may enter the major shrines at any hour of day or night without question. Once that has been accomplished, it will require tact, intelligence, stealth, and cunning to traverse the private regions of the complex and locate the suite wherein the flying monster is imprisoned. Thus, I suggest we recruit one whose face will not be known to the Temple staff, and certainly one who has not identified himself with the Throne Faction."

"Yes, it becomes better and better, my lord chamberlain," the Tyrant said, smiling craftily. "Now—where can we find such a man?"

"He stands before you, O King," said Janchan of Phaolon.

The Temple rose on the opposite side of the city from the palace enclosure. The streets were packed with carousing citizens, and every wineshop and alehouse and pleasure garden was crowded with celebrants on this Festival night. Janchan found it difficult to find a *zaiph* for public hire, but eventually he hailed one, paid its driver and, settling back in the rear saddle, let himself be flown across Ardha to where the squat Temple reared its height among lesser structures.

Tipping the driver liberally, and affecting a drunken stagger, Janchan drew the gaudy festival cape closely about him and lurched up the steps and into the central nave. Coils of incense floated on the air; votive lamps glowed like burning eyes through the gloom; the vast dome above echoed to the shuffle of many feet, the drone of priests, the mumbled prayers of hundreds of worshipers.

He worked his way around the subsidiary shrines which lay beyond the central nave, separated from the main hall by an arcade of ornate columns. Eventually he found one devoted to the Spider God that was dark and deserted. Without a moment's hesitation he whisked off his bright cape and tucked it beneath the black jerkin it had concealed. Then he drew the cowl tight about his features, pulled black gloves on his hands, and jumped up, clinging to the interstices of the further wall. He began to climb it, hand over hand.

It was not such a difficult feat as it sounds. The marble was pierced in ten thousand places in an elaborate fretwork that was like stone lace. Slipping through to the other side of the fretwork wall he began to ascend the outer surface of the enormous dome. There was very little danger of being seen, for the worshipers who thronged the cathedral-like nave beneath his heels were rapt on their devotions, and he would be hard to see, a crawling shadow in the dim gloom above their heads.

By the time he had ascended to the height of the third story, he crawled out along a spar of stone and descended the body of an enormous mythological caryatid, coming to the floor of a corridor. This part of the Temple, the King's councillors had told him, was private. Somewhere in this story or the one above he was most likely to find the winged creature locked away.

And the Princess Niamh as well ... but Akhmim knew nothing of his hopes in that direction. For Janchan had boldly planned to accomplish the freeing of two captives this night, not one!

The corridor was empty. It was also poorly lit, only a few fat tapers were surmounted by wavering flames, and these were too few and too far apart to do little more than merely alleviate the darkness. He slunk down the corridor on stealthy feet, using his mind to call telepathically to Zarqa.

When Onqqua had vocalized his plan to free the Kalood, and Akhmim had wondered aloud where they might find a loyal man unknown to the Temple Faction, Janchan had volunteered his services on the spur of the moment. At first the councillors were incredulous; then they realized that since he had only been in the service of Unggor for some twelve days, no one was likely to have even noticed his very existence as of yet. Akhmim, eyeing him shrewdly, demanded why a foreigner new to Ardha should so willingly volunteer for so dangerous a mission, since his loyalties were new and untested. Janchan had replied, with seeming candor, that he could hope for no better way to come to the favorable attention of the highest men in the realm than by succeeding in this task. He managed to get across the impression that he was an unscrupulous and ambitious young soldier-of-fortune, who meant to rise in the ranks as rapidly and as high as possible, and didn't fear to risk his skin in the ascent.

It was really this last point that won Akhmim's approval for the scheme. The Tyrant, an ambitious man of few scruples, admired these same qualitites in others; or, at least, could understand them, as he shared the same himself.

And so it was arranged. Raiment was chosen for him, money laid out, archivists roused from slumber to unroll maps of the Temple precincts for his quick scrutiny. He determined to attempt the deed that very night. To delay the attempt even another hour meant to stand idly by while the balance of power dipped ever more in Arjala's favor.

Akhmim liked that idea, too. With dawn, as his people stirred with aching heads and fuzzy tongues after the excesses of the night, they would rise to find his royal proclamation of Arjala's misconception of the heavenly decree blazoned on every wall and placard. . . .

Suddenly, Janchan froze motionlessly.

A sound of muffled sobbing came to him from beyond the door at which he had paused. Janchan knew that Zarqa was unequipped with vocal apparatus: yet there was desperation in that muffled weeping. On impulse he put his eye against the grating and peered within.

And saw Niamh the Fair, the long-sought Princess of Phaolon!

Chapter 19

WHEN COMRADES MEET

The door was a heavily carved and ornamented slab of wood—but it was barred from the *outside!* It was the work of an instant to slide back the bar, open the door, and slip within, closing it behind him.

Sprawled on a silken divan, Niamh glanced up suddenly. Her enormous and brilliant eyes widened with astonishment at the sight of this grim, black-clad phantom which had materialized out of the gloom. Then it raised black-clad hands to strip away the cloth that hid its features from her. And, to her utter amazement, they were the features of a man well known to her.

"Is is—can it be—?" she faltered.

The lithe young swordsman cast himself at her feet.

"It is Janchan of the Ptolnim who kneels at your feet, my Princess! Your servant—and your slave."

The girl was dazed, like one who wakens from sleep, yet is unsure as to whether she still dreams.

"Prince Janchan ... here?" she murmured in bewilderment.

"But one of the many of your court, my Princess, who have vowed themselves to unending quest until you are set free and returned to your throne unharmed," he said.

She raised slim wrists to press back her floating, silvery hair.

"But ... how have you come here, into the very citadel of my enemies?"

"My Princess—there is no time for questions now, and even less for answers! We must quickly leave this place, before my presence is discovered. Have you a cloak and hood to hide yourself?"

She gestured toward a wardrobe across the dim-lit room, saying there might be one within. He sprang to his feet and searched through its contents swiftly, drawing out a long, night-blue *narjeeb* which he bade her don, and quickly.

"I search for yet a second captive, who may be somewhere hereabouts," he said tersely. "Know you aught of a winged, gold-skinned man—"

"Do you mean the Kalood whom Arjala calls her *amphashand?*"

"The very same," Janchan said, grinning with relief. "Where is he held?"

The princess indicated a room on the story above. Janchan thought swiftly: to attempt to gain the upper story with the princess at his side might prove dangerous, and her presence an encumbrance to him if he should have to fight a guard. Perhaps it would be better to leave her here, bolting the door as before, and return to bear her to safety once Zarqa was freed. In swift, curt phrases he appraised her of his plan, and she agreed, tossing the voluminous *narjeeb* aside so it could be donned instantly at need.

"Does your chamber always go unguarded?" he asked. She answered that two guards stood at her door night and day, and that if they were missing tonight, it must be that Festival services must be overcrowded this night of all nights, drawing them to temporary duties elsewhere.

"And what of the Lord Chong?" he asked. "Was he captured with you, and is he imprisoned nearby?"

An expression of acute suffering passed across her perfect features; her exquisite eyes dimmed with tears.

"He . . . died, defending me, when we attempted our escape from the outlaws," she said in a low voice whose words he could hardly hear.

"Died? Gods—what a loss! The nation shares your sorrow at the demise of your champion, my Princess! But now I must be gone, for there is yet much to do and the night is all too short."

He saluted her and swiftly left the chamber, his heart high, exultant. He had hoped to find and free both Niamh and Zarqa . . . and it seemed the Gods were with him on this venture, in all truth!

The stairway leading to the floor above was as deserted as the corridor. Janchan ascended it, one hand on the hilt of his weapon. Without particular difficulty, he found the suite Niamh had indicated. The door thereof, also a massive slab of carved wood, was sealed with a heavy bar, which he slid aside.

Within he found Zarqa shackled to a bedpost. The sad-eyed Kalood evinced no surprise at his appearance, having detected the approach of Janchan through his telepathic senses.

The chains were of glassteel and thus unbreakable, but the bedpost itself was of wood and Janchan hacked through it with his sword with some little labor. Then it was an easy matter to slide the chains off. Zarqa rubbed his lean wrists gratefully.

My captors have imprisoned me in surroundings of considerable luxury, as you can see, he said. *Still, the caged dhua longs for its freedom, however golden the bars.*

Janchan smiled; Arjala had certainly lodged her heavenly prisoner in a sumptuous cell, for the walls were hung with jeweled draperies of rare silks, and goblets and dishes of sweetmeats and fruits stood about on taborets of precious woods inlaid with ivory mosaics. In a terse, low tone and few words Janchan apprised the Winged Man of the situation, and of his plans.

"So you must fly from here, recover the sky-sled, and return to take us aboard," he said urgently. "I hope your wing-wound has healed so that you are air-worthy by now, for it is hopeless to trust that we three can find our way out of the Temple precincts on foot, as easily as I got in."

Zarqa nodded solemnly. *The Temple physicians have lavished the extent of their healing arts upon my wing-joint, and, although my wings are stiff and lame from inactivity, I will, I trust, be able to fly a brief distance. But how will I recognize the window of the princess' suite?*

"We will leave a lamp burning within it," Janchan said. "One more thing occurs to me. With the two of us aboard, and Karn, and now the added weight of the princess, will the sky-sled be able to fly? I have no idea of its weight capacity. . . ." His voice trailed off at sight of the expression on Zarqa's face. "What's wrong?" he asked.

Normally glum, the Kalood's visage wore an expression of deepest sorrow.

You will not, I fear, have to worry about weight, the Winged Man telepathed. *The boy crept away in the night—the same night you left us. Perhaps I should have anticipated some such thing, for it was obvious how deeply he missed not being permitted to accompany you on this adventure.*

"Well, where is he?"

The Kalood gave an eloquent shrug. *I fear his spirit has fled to The World Above, as you would say. With dawn, when I discovered him missing, I searched through most of the tree. I found the signs of a struggle, and a great quantity of blood; but I did not find Karn.*

This was indeed grim news, and Janchan's heart saddened.

"You are not sure he's dead, though; he might, after all, have escaped victorious, and the blood you found could be the blood of the thing he fought."

Perhaps you are right. I certainly hope so. But, in any case, we have no idea where to begin looking for him, and to carry the Princess of Phaolon to safety must be our chiefest concern. With a roused and angry city stirred up like a zzumalak-nest on news of the rescue of the princess, we could hardly afford to hover about, searching for the lost boy.

"I suppose you are correct," Janchan said glumly. "Still, it is not right to just fly off and leave him to his own devices. After all, through him both you and I were freed from the captivity of Sarchimus. . . ."

I agree, the Kalood said sadly, *and I like the notion of leaving without certain knowledge that he is alive or dead no more than you. But I cannot help feeling that, somehow, he would understand. And, at all costs, we must get the princess free of the toils of Arjala.*

Janchan nodded; there was no question of this. They went over to Zarqa's window, which was barred with an ornamental grille of worked metal. Between the two of them it was not very difficult to pry the bars loose, employing the sawed bedpost as a lever. Soon they had widened sufficient space for the gaunt Kalood to squeeze through the bars.

Standing on the sill, Zarqa tested his wings gingerly once or twice, nodded his satisfaction, bade the prince farewell, and sailed off into the night.

Wiping the sweat from his brow, Janchan thought to himself that everything was going according to his plan—thus far, at any rate.

Chapter 20

THE THING AT THE WINDOW

Janchan stole from Zarqa's suite, barring the door behind him, and crept cautiously down the hall, and down the staircase, retracing his steps again to Niamh's door.

But this time, things were a trifle different.

Two guards stood to either side of the barred door. Whatever the reason why they had left their post before his earlier visit to the princess, here they were back again, and two ugly and dangerous-looking louts they were.

Temple Guards, he knew, were eunuchs trained in the more obscure techniques of hand-to-hand fighting, since bladed weapons were forbidden by religious law to Temple servitors. Ordinary guards in the Temple ranks circumvented this churchly fiat by going armed with whips or staves or cudgels. But not the Temple eunuchs, who fought with their bare hands.

Both men were bald and very heavy, and taller by a full hand-span than the lithe young princeling. Their hands were enormous and muscular and bore ridges of calloused skin. They wore loose felt vests over their hairless chests, and baggy pantaloons, secured at their thick waists with voluminous cummerbunds.

From the curve of the stairs he watched them, thinking fast. He could think of no reliable way of getting past them. He certainly couldn't talk his way through that wall of living flesh, and he was not at all certain he could get past them, even if he used his sword. He was reluctant to attempt a battle in any case—not because they were two to his one, but because they would undoubtedly raise a loud outcry, summoning help from below.

On impulse, he went back to the floor on which Zarqa had been imprisoned. Assuming the number of apartments along the hall was the same on this floor as it was on the

141

floor below, he conceived of the daring scheme of climbing down the outer wall of the Temple and entering Niamh's suite via the window.

Cautiously, he stole into the suite that was directly above Niamh's; luckily, it was unoccupied. Even more to the point, the window was unbarred. Obviously, the grille had been affixed to Zarqa's window because of the danger of his escaping through flight. Ordinarily, it seemed, there was no reason in barring windows so high off the branch.

He stripped the bed of its satin spread, which he quickly cut into long strips with his blade, knotting these together into a makeshift rope. It was lengthy enough, he thought; it remained to be seen, however, whether or not it was strong enough to bear his weight without tearing or coming untied.

Winding one end around a pilaster of marble, he tossed the rest of the line out the open window, swung over the sill, took a firm hold of it, and let go with his feet.

Giddily, he swung through space, far above the paved forum below. Looking down, he was disconcerted to discover how high in the air he actually was. But he was not much disconcerted by the giddy height; like all Laonese, Janchan was immune to acrophobia.

Slowly he swung down, hand over hand..

The wind caught his cloak and spread it like black wings.

The pavement swung to and fro, two hundred feet under his heels.

The descent was not as difficult as it might have been. For one thing, the outer wall of the Temple was covered with carved ornament, which afforded him a variety of footholds. For another, he did not have to climb far, as the stories at this height were only about twenty-five feet apart.

At length his heel rasped against the stone of Niamh's sill. Wooden shutters locked away the night wind, but he broke them open easily enough, and climbed in to greet the astonished girl.

The excitement of the promised rescue whipped color into her cheeks and brought a sparkle to her eyes. She laughed a bit excitedly.

"Last time you came in by the door; this time, by the window. What will it be next time—the flue of the chimney?"

He grinned, but laid a finger across his lips, enjoining her to silence.

"The guards are back outside your door," he whispered. "Have you a lamp?"

"A lamp?" She frowned uncertainly.

He nodded and she fetched one, a hollowed sphere of lucent alabaster, filled with oil. At his gesture, she lighted the wick and he took it in both hands to set it on the windowsill, handing her the sword to hold.

A sound behind them—the rasp of sandal-leather.

They turned. The door stood open, and within the portal stood a tall woman between the two eunuchs. It would be hard to say which party was the most surprised.

The woman was superb and voluptuous, with full breasts cupped in sparkling blue *jaonce* and a girdle of strung pearls clasping her waist and draped across her swelling thighs. A bright red gem glittered in her navel, and her silky hair, faintly luminous with gold highlights, was woven through with small metal bells which chimed sweetly as she tossed her head, tiara flashing.

She stared at them incredulously. Under arched brows, her eyes were wells of amber flame, and her lips were full, moistly scarlet. She was remarkably beautiful, but her face was cold, proud, imperious, and lacked the softness and warmth that could have made it womanly.

It was, of course, Holy Arjala. Janchan was never to know what had impelled her to come to Niamh's chamber on this night of Festival; suffice it to say that she had come at the worst possible time. For now her nostrils flared, her face whitened with fury, and she gestured with a small ceremonial jeweled whip.

The huge eunuchs lumbered forward, their calloused hands swinging from anthropoid shoulders, lamplight gleaming on their oiled torsos.

Janchan was disarmed. He had handed his sword to Niamh, while taking up the lamp. And now it was out of reach, for at the sight of the Goddess Incarnate the princess had shrunk back against the window.

He had nothing to fight with but the heavy bowl of alabaster, filled with liquid fire. So he hurled it at the first eunuch just as the huge creature sprang at him with a soundless snarl, massive paws flashing for his throat, to crush and maim.

The bowl caught him on the skull like a hammer-blow

and shattered his skull. It, too, shattered, and rivulets of flaming oil ran across the floor in every direction. The heavy draperies with which the walls were hung went up in a sheet of flame; the heavily waxed parquet flooring ignited in a flash, and within a few seconds the room was a roaring inferno.

Arjala had leaped to the left of her eunuch when the lamp struck him, and she was now within reach of Janchan. She whirled on him, her face ablaze with fury, and struck out with the little jeweled whip. He seized it, twisted it from her hand, and flung her from him. She reeled back and fell against a table, striking her head. She lay there, stunned, a trickle of blood leaking down between her breasts from a small cut on her brow.

The second eunuch still lived, but there was nothing he could do, for a wall of seething flame now divided him from his mistress and the two they had surprised in attempting to escape.

He turned and ran from the room. But he did not call out to rouse the guards on the lower levels, which was peculiar. The answer flashed into Janchan's mind, and he grinned slightly.

The Temple surgeons had cut more from the two eunuchs than just their gender. Janchan uttered a grim, ironic laugh. All of this mess had come about because he thought it too dangerous to try to cut down the guards with his blade, because he feared they would yell for assistance and rouse the place.

But they had been tongueless mutes, all the while!

They were doomed, of course. The room was a blinding furnace by now. Waves of heat baked them, singeing the floating silken locks of the princess and scorching the edges of Janchan's cloak. They could escape the flames only by leaping from the window to the distant tiles far below. It was certain death; still, it was faster and cleaner than what they would face if they stayed here. For here they would be burned alive.

Suddenly, Janchan thought of the dangling satin cord whereby he had climbed down from the floor above! It still dangled before the open window, and by it perhaps they could climb to a higher level. It might thrust them into the hands of Temple Guards, for the halls must be alive with them by now, but even capture was preferable to death.

He bent to take up the limp body of Arjala. Enemy or not, he could not leave her here to die in the flames. That was too terrible a death to envision for one so beautiful, and he was too innately chivalrous to leave the helpless woman to such a doom.

Behind him, Niamh crouched against the window, staring into the flames.

Suddenly, from behind, a great clawed hand touched her shoulder, and she whirled about to stare into a weirdly inhuman face that peered down at her like something from a nightmare.

As its claws clutched her by the shoulders she screamed.

Part 5

THE BOOK
OF KLYGON
THE ASSASSIN

Chapter 21

WINGED HORROR

In these events I did not, of course, partake. I knew utterly nothing of them at the time, and it was not until very much later that I heard enough of the separate adventures of Zarqa and Janchan to reconstruct them; which reconstruction I have recorded here, so that these chronicles will be as complete and perfect as my poor skill can make them.

On that night when Prince Janchan left us to venture alone into the Yellow City, I lay awake, staring into the darkness, bitterly bemoaning my fate. That it should be by the hand of another that my beloved princess should be set free was intolerable to me and I viewed the notion with loathing.

At length I rose and silently dressed myself in warriors' trappings and gathered up my gear, borrowing certain of the instruments which Zarqa had purloined from the Scarlet Pylon, and filling my pouch with the precious coins we had taken from the coffers of Sarchimus. Then I crept out of the tent of leaves into the darkness where the gaunt and faithful Kalood lay sleeping soundly on his pallet.

I could not endure the thought that it should be another who should rescue the woman I loved from peril, and not I myself. Prince Janchan was my tried and loyal friend, and a man of honor and chivalry, but I came close to hating him there in the secret watches of the night. That he should perform brave and gallant deeds before the admiring eyes of Niamh the Fair made me quiver with impotent fury.

I told myself that it was unfair to expect him to go forward alone into danger, that one other should stand beside him to make the fight more equal. Now I laugh grimly at my pathetic and foolish attempts to pretend I crept from

the camp from noble and altruistic motives. By such igno-
ble means does the human heart delude itself, feeding on
lies; for it was a lover's jealousy alone that goaded me
into the night—jealousy that another should win the admiration and thanks of the woman I loved.

I began to descend the slope of the branch. I know now
that I should have left behind a note for Zarqa to find at
dawn, when he roused and came to waken me and found
me gone. I try to pretend that it was only because I
lacked writing implements that I did not leave a note for
him; but the answer is, quite simply, that my mind was a
seething maelstrom of jealous fantasies and I never once
thought of it.

It is at night that the terrible predators of the Green
Star World emerge from nest and lair to hunt their prey.
So, of course, I got into serious trouble before I had been
gone from the camp more than half an hour.

I was striding down a small branchlet toward the crotch
of the great tree when I stumbled into a small, grim
drama.

An immense monster bee was slaying a grub.

The bee was the size of a full-grown bull, and many times
as dangerous. Its glittering oval wings were like sheets
of veined opal and its furred body glistened with an oily
sheen. The grub was a huge soft sluglike thing and the
stinger of the bee had run it through the belly. It bled co-
piously, red gore splattering the branch in every direction,
and despite the gaping wound it yet lived and clung to the
stinger which transfixed it, flopping and squirming slowly.

At my approach, the monster bee turned upon me a
glittering and soulless gaze. Eyes like immense, faceted jet
beads stared as if seeking to ascertain if my approach indicated danger. The dim, small intellect behind the glistening helm of horny black chitin doubtless assumed I meant
to rob it of the fat grub that was intended for its nocturnal meal. I, of course, desired only to pass and continue
on my way.

However, the branch was rounded here, and fell away
in a giddy curve to either side of where the enormous insect squatted above its prey. I could not easily pass to either side, without danger of falling from the branch. So I
stood there, waiting for the bee to bear away its dinner.

That was, it proved, exactly the wrong thing to have
done under the circumstances. For my motionless presence

roused vague suspicions of my harmlessness in the minus-
cule intellect of the predator. It turned from the dying
grub to face me on the branch, its stalked and many-
jointed limbs scissoring as it wheeled about. I saw the
honey-sacs on its rear limbs as it changed position, and
knew that this must be none other than one of the creatures Zarqa had referred to as a *zzumalak*.

Then it hurled itself upon me with blurring speed.

The *zzumalak* flashed at me like a charging tiger, and
for a fatal fraction of a second I was too surprised to
move or even flinch.

Dry, clawed mandibles seized me up, coarse-bristled
forelimbs brushing against my bare thighs. In the next second my sword was out and I was fighting for my very life,
there in the dense gloom, on the insecure footing of a
blood-splattered and perilously narrow branch.

The deadly sting was a tapering needle of black horn
thrice the length of my arm. It stabbed at me with blind-
ingly swift, convulsive thrusts. Karn's muscles and reflexes were those of a trained hunter, but he knew little of
the formal art of fencing. But my mind was that of a
trained swordsman, and I remembered much of the skill
that had been instinctive to me when I dwelt in the body
of Kyr Chong. So we were not unevenly matched.

It was an eerie duel, there on the high, swaying branch,
amid the leafy darkness—man against monster bee—
sword against sting. I parried every stroke with desperate
skill, using every trick of the art of fencing I knew. Again
and again my agile point slid past the monster's guard and
my blade sank deep into its curving flanks or thick-furred
belly. But the *zzumalak* seemed utterly insensitive to pain
and did not tire or slow, although the oily ooze that was
its vital fluid leaked slowly from many puncture-wounds.

I had hacked away two of its clutching limbs, but one
great claw still clutched me, caught in the leather straps of
my trappings. Thus it was that when the *zzumalak* rose
suddenly into the air on drumming wings, I went with it.

I was lucky, though. Dangerous as my position had now
become, it could easily have been worse. Those sharp
claws could have been sunk deep in my belly. . . .

As the *zzumalak* rose into the air the dying grub wriggled over the incline of the branchlet and fell. Thus it was
that with dawn when Zarqa came searching for some

trace of me, he found only the blood shed by the grub, but no grub, and formed the natural assumption that the gore was my own.

Either from the burden of my weight or from some internal injury my blade had caused, the *zzumalak* wavered drunkenly in its flight. Wings of sheeted opal drummed unsteadily, falteringly, and the monster bee hurtled across the span between the tree whereon we had battled and its neighbor. This, by a lucky chance, was the tree in which the city of Ardha was built; but it might easily have been another.

The winged horror tipped, staggering in its flight, and began to lose altitude. I clung to the forelimb whose claws were caught in my harness, lest the wounded brute should release its grasp on me and I should fall into the abyss.

The wind whistled about me, whirling my cloak and tugging at my hair. The sickening depths of the abyss below swung giddily. The lamps of Ardha were nearer now.

My position was incalculably dangerous. I clung desperately with one hand to the bristled, horny limb of the injured *zzumalak*, my other hand still clenching the hilt of my sword, which I dared not lose.

At any instant the flying predator might falter in its flight and fall, bearing me with it to a horrible doom in the unthinkable abyss miles below.

Or it might well soar on past Ardha, carrying me countless leagues away from the Yellow City which was my goal.

And there was absolutely nothing I could do to alter the situation to the slightest degree in my favor. I could, I suppose, have thrust my blade deep into the thorax of the flying thing from beneath, hoping to strike a vulnerable organ. But that, of course, would merely precipitate me into the abyss.

The lights of Ardha were below me now. I glimpsed torchlit processions streaming through the boulevards of the city, and lantern-lit gardens, and the lighted windows of the mansions and palaces. The *zzumalak* flew an erratic, meandering course across the breadth of the metropolis, wavering drunkenly in its flight.

My one-handed grip on its foreleg was loosening as my hand wearied. Risking much, I released my grip in order to hold my scabbard steady while I sheathed my sword, which would bree both hands for the task of clinging ahold of my unpredictable steed.

And then the *zzumalak* dropped me and I fell like a stone.

Chapter 22

BLACK MASKS IN THE NIGHT

Perhaps I cried out as I fell; I have no idea, for, if I did, the wind whipped the cry from my lips.

The instinct that bids a doomed man cling to life is a powerful one. For I reached out desperately with both arms to catch some obstacle and break my fall.

To my own amazement I caught hold of a slender shaft of wood.

At the time I had no idea of what it was. Now, looking back on my memories of that terrible, endless moment of falling through space, I think it must have been one of the long, slim flagstaffs that thrust from the rooftops of Ardhanese buildings and from which heraldic banners are suspended.

My hands struck it—slipped—and clung. The pole bent nearly double, and then broke away under my hurtling weight. And again I fell, but slower now, for the momentary impediment had broken the impetus of my fall.

Then I caromed into a vast, curved panel of fabric that must have been some sort of an awning. The strong cloth boomed under the impact of my fall, then tore free from its frame. But it, too, had served to partially break my fall.

And the next instant I struck a sheet of ice-cold water and lost my senses. Seconds later I rose to the surface, stunned, half-drowned, but somehow alive and in one piece. Groggily, I struck out for the marble lip of the pool, and dragged myself over, to flop onto the thick cushion of a flower-bed. I lay there while the world spun dizzily around me, then I levered myself up on one elbow and vomited out the water I had swallowed. I must have swallowed half the pool, at least; I hope the keeping of goldfish was not an Ardhanese custom!

Then, somewhat recovered, I got unsteadily to my feet and looked around me in the gloom.

I stood amid a formal, rooftop garden on one of the tiers of a princely mansion. Unfamiliar miniature trees rose about me; flower-beds lay underfoot, and patches of grassy sward, and meandering walks strewn with chips of fragrant wood instead of gravel.

Colored paper lanterns swung overhead, suspended in long garlands hung from tree to tree. By their dim, multi-colored illumination I could see the gleam of marble fountains and alabaster statuary. Ornamental gazebos rose amid trimmed hedges and grotesquely shaped topiary trees. Benches of glimmering crystal stood here and there upon the velvet lawn. It was most obvious that the *zzumalak* had dropped me into the roof garden of some noble's mansion, for such an aerial pleasance denoted wealth and luxury.

And that implied the presence of guards. Any intruder caught stealing about the roof gardens by night would assuredly be thought a thief or an assassin. I had best leave at once, I thought. Thus far my precipitous descent into the garden pool had gone unnoticed. But my luck would not last forever. Keeping well to the shadows and avoiding, where possible, the glowing paper lanterns that bobbed and swayed overhead, I prowled in search of a way out of here.

A flight of marble stairs caught my eye, the glimmer of light on its glossy balustrade. I headed toward it, through the scented trees. It led to a higher level, another rooftop, no doubt; perhaps from there I could jump or climb to the roof of an adjoining building. But how I was to get down to the street level without risking discovery by descending within one of these buildings I had no idea. Cursing the Ardhanese for their lack of fire escapes, I went swiftly up the stair to the higher level and found myself on a huge balcony faced with long glassed windows like French doors. Drapes were drawn before these windows, but the rooms beyond were brilliantly lit.

With my heart in my mouth and my drawn sword in my hand, I crossed the length of the balcony and found myself at the head of a second stair, identical in every respect to the one by which I had ascended. It led down to the roof garden again. I turned and looked up. The roof of this building was about twenty-five feet above me. The exterior of the building was of carved stone, worked into frowning masks and mythological figures which afforded an easy purchase for my hands and feet. Sheathing my blade again, I reached up, seized the shoulders of a stone caryatid, and began to climb.

I had come from the pool soaked and dripping, my dark cloak a soggy mass, my boots squelching underfoot. The dry air, the night wind, and my brisk exertions were rapidly drying me. So I scaled the wall with little difficulty, levered myself up over the roof-ledge, and found myself among a forest of chimneys and skylights. By now I was thoroughly lost, and further from the street level than when I had hauled myself out of that pool; but at least I was still undiscovered.

Not for long, however.

Four masked figures stepped from behind a tall chimney and pointed their daggers at me in ghostly silence.

I froze. There wasn't much else I could do, for I stood on the edge of the roof and my footing was precarious. So, cursing inwardly, I let them take my blade.

Whatever they were, they were obviously not guards, for their features were concealed behind visors of black silk, through whose slits their eyes glittered warily. They wore close-fitting garments, also of black, supple gloves, and light, voluminous capes of black silken stuff. They ran gloved hands over me swiftly and lightly, found my purse, and detached it from my girdle.

One of the masked men loosened the drawstring and poured the contents of the purse into his cupped palm. Precious metals sparkled in the distant lamplight, as the coins we had taken from the coffers of Sarchimus, with which I had stuffed my purse, poured from the pouch.

The masked man smiled—almost, I thought, approvingly.

"Unusual to find a clever thief in one so young," he said dryly. He poured the coins back it into my pouch which he then tucked away in a pocket on the inner lining of his cloak.

"Take him," he said, and they were upon me.

The masked men fought in complete silence and mastered me in a trice. Their clever hands knew the location of the nerve centers of my body, and I suffered excruciating pain for an instant; in the next, my limbs were numb and paralyzed.

Thongs tightened about my wrists; they drew my ankles together and lashed them tight. Then a peculiar harness was drawn about my torso, with a long silken cord attached to it. I was too dazed at the swiftness of all this to wonder at this cord, but in the next instant it became clear to me.

For they pushed me off the roof!

And, for the second time in the same hour, I hurtled down to smash against the street below—

But not quite! For the line attached to the harness drew taut. It checked my fall, crushing the air from my lungs. And I bounced and spun a few feet above the paven way, dangling at the end of the silken line.

I had fallen into a narrow, crooked, unlit alleyway. Now more masked men in black garments and cloaks melted out of the gloom to swarm about me. A knife flashed as one of them cut through the line. Strong arms caught me as the line loosened, easing me to the cobbles.

From where I lay on my back, staring up, I saw the masked men swinging lithely down the line from the roof above. In a few moments they landed lightly on the cobbles. The leader uttered a curt command. His men scooped me up and one sturdy rogue tossed me over his broad shoulders. They melted back into the shadows and moved silently and swiftly as the wind through unbroken darkness to an unknown destination.

What they wanted of me I did not know. Nor could I conjecture what my fate would be at their hands. But one thing I did know; and the knowledge was disquieting.

I had thought them thieves—as they had thought me.

But they were not thieves.

They were assassins!

Assassination is a peculiarly Laonese institution, and on the Green Star World they have raised the craft to the level of the fine arts. Clever, cunning men, trained in the disciplines of stealth and silence and secret murder, more than one of the jewel-box cities of this strange and wondrous planet has fallen beneath the dominance of the black-masked men.

In Phaolon, I knew, their guild had been broken generations before, and they had been driven forth. But here in Ardha, as I now surmised and would soon learn for certain, the Assassins' Guild was a third power, and close in wealth and strength and influence to Temple and Throne.

My heart beat low. From the frying pan to the fire! From the clutches of one of the monstrous predators of the forest, I had fallen into the hands of the most dangerous and feared and murderous men in the world. And what they wanted of me I could not even guess. . . .

Our rush through darkness had been silent and swift. We came to a halt before a massive wall of ancient stonework that soared out of sight overhead. One black-cloaked man bent forward and touched a hidden spring. A portion of the wall sank soundlessly into the ground, and a black opening gaped.

The leader of the band looked at me.

"Vial number two," he said quietly.

A black-gloved hand bore a small glass tube to my face and crushed it beneath my nose. I inhaled a pungent fluid that filled my head with piercing and aromatic vapors.

Then, in single file, stepping silently as cats, the Assassins vanished one by one into the black opening in the wall.

The burly-shouldered rogue bore me within as well.

But by then I knew nothing of my surroundings, nor of what occurred from that moment.

For the fluid in the vial had done its work, and I was unconscious.

Chapter 23

THE HOUSE OF GURJAN TOR

Perhaps an hour later I awoke in a barren, poorly-lighted room. I awoke instantly, coming from deepest slumber to full wakefulness without passing through the transitional phases. I felt perfectly comfortable, with no signs of headache or nausea or any other side effects of the drug. I smiled grimly; the Assassins of Ardha were remarkably adept in the pharmaceutical arts.

I rose to my feet from the pallet upon which I had awakened and looked about the room. The ceiling was raftered, with bare plaster between the rafters; the walls were wood paneling laid over what seemed to be solid stone. At least, thumping my balled fist at various places here and there on the walls, selected at random, I found no difference in sound that might suggest the presence of a secret panel.

Which was quite odd, for the room had neither windows nor door, and I had no idea how I had been brought in here, nor how my captors had left the room.

The floor was bare wood, inlaid with elaborate parquetry; this was the only note of ostentatious ornament about the chamber, which was otherwise quite Spartan in its rigorous simplicity. There were no hangings on the walls, no carpets on the floors, and no furnishings of any kind, save for the simple pallet in the corner, and a low sitting-bench, and a small wooden taboret which bore a single candle in a crystal dish.

There was, however, a jug of water, a cup of polished horn which was filled with a clear red wine, and a plate containing coarse brown bread and pickled meats. I was quite famished by this time—it must have been early morning by now—so I ate hungrily, and quenched my thirst.

The Assassins had taken nothing from me except my weapons. So I still bore over my shoulder a coil of the Live Rope we had carried off from the tower of Sarchimus, the vial of Liquid Flame, and my personal gear.

Even my purse had been returned to me, still filled with coins. The Assassins, it would seem, were no thieves.

The mystery of the doorless room intrigued me; search as I might, however, I could find no secret panel in the walls, nor were there any signs of a trap visible in the ceiling.

To pass the time I exercised, working up a good sweat. At length I rested from my exertions, drank some water, and finally, from sheer boredom as much as anything, stretched out on the pallet and napped.

Something awoke me an indiscernible period of time later. I lay without moving, lifting my lids a fraction of an inch, peering about me in the dimness. The candle had almost burned down, and the wick was guttering, old wax fuming, giving off a vile, greasy stench.

My skin prickled and uneasiness went through me. I cannot say how I knew it, but I felt inwardly certain that someone was watching me from a place of concealment. I lay still, my breast rising and falling with my breathing, feigning slumber. The pressure of invisible eyes were upon me; it was an uncanny sensation.

Suddenly a faint creaking sound came to my ears. Slitting my eyes, I peered at my feet. A square portion of the parquetry wherewith the floor was inlaid sank out of sight, and a man in black clambered lithely up from the opening.

So *that's* how they worked the trick! The secret entrance to my cell was not in either ceiling or walls, but in the floor. And that explained as well the unusually ornamental floor decoration, for the complex patterns of inlaid, subtly contrasting woods, concealed the edges of the hidden trap.

The man stood motionlessly, watching me for a long moment. He was a small man, stunted, with bowed legs. Beneath his black silken visor, his face was long-jawed, knobby, and remarkably ugly. I recognized him as one of the men in the band that had captured me on the rooftop, for there was no concealing those bowed legs.

Then he came over to the pallet and shook me by one

bare shoulder. I pretended to come awake with a great
start and stared up at him with an assumed expression of
bewilderment.

He chuckled.

"Frightened you, lad? Naught to fear ... yet, at any
rate." His voice was hoarse—I had later to learn his fond-
ness for strong, unwatered wine—and he had an indescribable accent I can only describe as the Laonese equivalent
of Cockney.

I jumped to my feet.

"What do you want with me?"

"Well, first of all, your name," he said, seating himself
on my little bench. I gave it.

"Karn ... 'tis not an Ardhan name," he said, rolling the
name on his tongue as if tasting it. I acknowledged that it
was not.

"Be you a member of the Thieves' Guild, then?" he
asked, naming a small competitor of his own Guild, with
which a certain contention existed for control of the crim-
inal underworld in the city. I told him that I was not.

"Who is your master?"

"I have none."

"Your parents, then?"

"No parents, either."

He rubbed a long, big-knuckled hand along his knobby
jaw.

"Do you know where you are?"

"I assume this to be the headquarters of the Assassins'
Guild," I said.

He nodded. Then: "This is the house of Gurjan Tor,"
he said impressively.

"And who might Gurjan Tor be?" I asked indifferently.

"He is the chief of the Guild and the most celebrated of
all Assassins," he said.

"Well, if he's that important, what does he want with a
mere boy?" I asked bluntly.

He grinned cheerfully, displaying a remarkable set of
broken and decayed teeth.

"A reasonable question, lad; aye, reasonable. And I'll
say this by way of answer: he just might have a purpose
for a lad as young as you who has the guts and the wits to
rob the Ispycian Palace alone and unaided, carrying off a
fistful of rare and precious antique coins. ..."

I said nothing. This was the first inkling I had gained

that the coins from the coffers of Sarchimus were more than common legal tender.

The bowlegged little man shook his head admiringly.

"Yes, I'll hand it to you, lad, it showed a clear head and good sense. Most lads would be too inexperienced, or too afeared, or both, to spot the value of them coins. Why, they'd try to lug off a man's-weight of tapestry or an *abrium* statuette, and would trip over their own feet in getting away. But, no, you picked the most valuable items of their size and compactness—next best things to gems, which would be locked in the vaults, anyway. For which reason, it's Gurjan Tor himself would see you now, so come along. . . ."

Without further ado the comical little man led me down through the floor and into a maze of tunnels from which we soon emerged into dim-lit and unadorned corridors.

As I followed him, I speculated on my fate. Perhaps I might get out of this alive, after all!

And I thanked my lucky stars I had paused to fill my pouch with coins. . . .

The house of the Assassins was a dark, empty, gloomy place, filled with shadows and whispers and unseen eyes. My guide led me into a rather large room, as Spartan and devoid of decorations as the one in which I had awakened, save for a large divan in its exact center.

It was immense, this divan, and thickly strewn with glittering silks, luxurious furs, and many plump pillows. Thereupon reclined the fattest man I have ever seen. He must have weighed five hundred pounds if he weighed an ounce, and his obesity was repulsive and almost frightening, like a deformity. He was stark naked to boot, with a sumptuous velvet robe thrown casually about him, and through its front his vast paunch and wobbling, womanish breasts gleamed with an oily dew. It was perfume, I realized as I approached his silken nest. He was literally soaked in the stuff, and it was all I could do to breathe.

Amid this tangled bed of furs and jeweled silks and fat pillows, Gurjan Tor squatted like a bloated and obscene toad. From a low taboret of precious metals he was gobbling tidbits of wine-soaked meat. His little slitted eyes watched me, cold and shrewd and calculating, as I made the required obeisance. But neither then nor at any point during the interview did he for a moment cease slobbering over the greasy meats.

He was completely bald, his yellow moon-face inscrutable, save for the eyes. They were black as ink, and cold as ice. And they seemed to look through me to the very roots of my soul.

In few, terse words the bowlegged little man who had fetched me reported on his questioning of me. What he had to say seemed to please Gurjan Tor, for he smiled. Still stuffing his mouth with juicy gobbets, he inquired of me in a soft, high-pitched, almost feminine voice of my expertise in the use of certain weapons, of my experience in the several arts of stealth, and of my origin.

I told him what I truthfully could; and, as for my non-existent career in thievery, I made up what details I could invent which sounded plausible.

Again, my answers seemed to please him.

"You speak with the accents of Phaolon," he observed shrewdly, "yet claim birth among the forest barbarians: how is that?"

I was already perspiring, and this did not help my equanimity any, as you might imagine. For one thing I had never actually realized the Laonese spoke with regional accents.

I shrugged, attempting to appear unruffled. "My parents may have come from that city, for all I know," I said. "Many are they whom the monarchs of the various cities have driven into exile among the forest-wandering tribesmen. . . ."

"True enough," he said in his high, sweet voice. Then, addressing the bowlegged man, who had doffed his visor upon entering the room in what was obviously accepted social custom among the Assassins, he said:

"Klygon, I am pleased. This youth shall be enlisted among the novices at once, and placed in training for Project Three. See to it."

We backed from the Presence. The fat man did not deign to notice, having turned his full attention to a tray of sweets.

Chapter 24

I LEARN THE ARTS OF STEALTH

And thus I became an Assassin. Or a novice in training, at any rate. And my friend, mentor, master, and comrade was to be none other than Klygon the Sly, as he was called. For, as Master of the Novices, it was his task to teach and train the young apprentices of the Guild in the secret arts.

Klygon was a hard man not to like. His humor was sly and infectious, and his enthusiasm for assassinry—or whatever you might wish to call it—was that of a master artisan for his craft. The ugly, comical little man was an unsparing taskmaster, true, but he was wise and witty, generous and loyal. I grew fond of him.

I grew also to become a trained and experienced Assassin, and in less time than it seemed possible. I had been selected for one particular task—the mysterious "Project Three" of which Gurjan Tor had spoken—and my every waking moment for the next twelve days was devoted to the acquisition of the skills I should require for this task.

We rose at dawn and for two hours before breakfast Klygon drilled us in the formal and informal arts of swordplay. The formal arts consisted of those of the courtly *duello;* you might call it the art of fence. As I sorely lacked instruction in this science—so indispensable to one who desires to continue living in a world filled with ferocious monsters and no less savage human adversaries—I soaked up everything Klygon could teach me with great interest. As for what I have termed the informal arts of swordplay, these were the dirty tricks of rough-and-tumble street-fighting, the skills of the gutter.

After breakfast, as if we were not already aching from sore muscles, we exercised in a huge vaulted cellar-like chamber. Here Klygon taught us how to fall and tumble and roll and bounce back up, how to scale ropes, run on ladders, use line and grapnel, climb surfaces so smooth that even the nimblest monkey might find it difficult to seek a toehold. We learned also how to tread as soundlessly as a cat: first on a bare floor full of creaking boards, then on a darkened stair littered with pots and pans, and finally on a bed of crisp, dry leaves. No Mohawk on the warpath could slink through the forest aisles as silently as I, when I completed this phase of my training.

Normally, I was given to understand, the pace of Klygon's tutelage was more leisurely. In my case the pace was accelerated almost beyond human endurance, and all because of the impending Project Three, whose hour was rapidly approaching.

I began to pick up bits and pieces of information, which I fitted together one by one. In the first place, I learned that there was much more to being an Assassin than just learning how to kill silently and swiftly. Of a certainty the Assassins of Ardha killed political opponents on commission; but they also dealt in kidnapping, in blackmail, and in the theft and sale of secrets.

There is probably no need for me to say, that, in the matter of becoming a novice of the Assassins, I had no choice; in fact, my wishes were not even consulted. The decision was that of Gurjan Tor alone. It was either accept and make the best of it, or die in any one of a number of less-than-pleasant ways. For once you have entered the house of Gurjan Tor, and have been admitted to the secret circle of the Assassins, there is no leaving it, save as a member of the Guild, or feet forward, as the saying goes. So I perforce became an Assassin.

The political situation here in Ardha was singularly complex, I learned. For years a three-way power-struggle between Throne, Temple, and Guild had all but rent the kindom asunder into sharply divided factions.

Some time ago, when the Tyrant delivered his ultimatum of marriage or war at the court of Niamh the Fair, he had held the central position of power. But the failure of that attempt, and his subsequent failure to either bring Phaolon to its knees or mount an army of invasion, had considerably weakened his grasp on the reins of power. The failure to launch an invasion, I now learned, was due simply to a lack of funds.

Seeing the power of the Throne Faction eclipsed, Holy Arjala the Goddess Incarnate had made her bold strike for power. Yielding the Temple revenues for one year to Gurjan Tor had won her the temporary allegiance of the Guild to her side; and thus the balance of power tipped from Throne to Temple. It was Arjala's ultimate ambition to share the throne of Akhmim, thus uniting the power of both factions into a single cause. This had been done, incidentally, in Phaolon much earlier; in the reign of Niamh's father, Throne and Temple had aligned in marriage, and my beloved princess was herself considered the Goddess Incarnate in her realm, as well as queen thereof. But the Phaolonians represent a higher and more sophisticated level of civilization than the backward and warlike race of Ardha; in Phaolon, the national religion was a social custom, to which lip service was paid, but it exerted little power and little authority over the minds of the citizenry; not so in Ardha.

Of this new alignment of power in Ardha, Gurjan Tor was wary. The Goddess has bought his allegiance, but not, it would seem, for long. I think the cunning leader of the Assassins feared, and not without good reason, that once Arjala and Akhmim had united their factions, they would turn upon the Guild and destroy it, thus eliminating the only potential disruptive factor in their midst.

In other words, the old double-cross was coming.

But Gurjan Tor planned to get there first.

The days crept by slowly, and I chafed to see valuable time elude me. For all I knew, every hour brought Prince Janchan nearer to his goal of rescuing the Princess of Phaolon. And he was free to act at will, to come and go as he pleased, with no restraints on his movements (insofar as I knew), while I was a prisoner of the Assassins.

It was infuriating. But, frankly, Klygon kept me so busy from dawn to dark, that I really had little opportunity to consider these matters. All day I trained in the wearisome arts of stealth; at night I crept into my bed bone-weary from sheer exhaustion, and my slumbers were deep and without dreams.

As yet I neither knew nor suspected anything of the nature of the mysterious Project Three for which I had been selected. When I inquired of Klygon concerning it, the bowlegged little man looked uncomfortable and muttered something or other to the effect that I would know in due time.

"But I want to know now," I complained.

"Be a good lad," he advised, "and it'd be wise if you troubled yourself naught about it."

"But why is it being kept a secret from me?" I demanded.

He shrugged, and lowered his voice to a conspiratorial whisper.

" 'Tis the will of Gurjan Tor that the scheme be kept secret, lad. And you'd be better to learn now that *no one* goes against the will of Gurjan Tor! Not if he wants to keep on breathing, he don't. . . ."

So I held my peace and applied myself to my training, but kept my eyes and ears open all the same. The days passed slowly and I prospered in my studies. Klygon, who regarded his craft with the affection and enthusiasm and dedication a connoisseur feels for his favorite art, shook his head admiringly at my progress as I displayed my newly-acquired skills before him.

"Aye, lad, you do me proud; and I doubt not that even Gurjan Tor would think you a real credit to your teacher!"

But he still wouldn't tell me what it was all about.

The Flower Boat Festival neared. This annual day and night of carnival was celebrated with great festivities by the folk of Ardha. And it occurred to me more than once, as the deadline for the termination of my training grew nearer and it could be seen that it was obviously planned to coincide with the great national festival, that on such a night a deed of stealth would have the greatest possible chance of success. With the boulevards and avenues thronged with celebrants, every wineshop and pleasure garden filled with citizens, the guardsmen would have their hands full and their work cut out for them.

This had also occurred to Gurjan Tor.

Festival day dawned. I saw nothing of the day-long processions, the flower-barges drawn by matched teams of *zaiphs* or *dhua;* locked away in the secret citadel of the Guild, I did not even know of Arjala's magnificent coup as she sprung the existence of her bewinged and celestial captive, Zarqa the Kalood, on an astounded populace and a

completely confounded Akhmim. But word of this reached
the central room where Gurjan Tor squatted like some
bloated and obscene toad in his silken nest. And Klygon
and I were again summoned into the Presence.

On this occasion the half-naked fat man was gorging on
slivers of pickled fishmeat as we entered the bare and
gloomy chamber and rendered him our obeisance.

With a silver skewer he indicated a wall-chart.

"The boy must be ready tonight," he squeaked in his
high-pitched, feminine voice. "And an hour earlier than
planned. Matters have changed, perhaps for the better.
Yonder chart shows the inner structure of the Temple; the
red cross-mark indicates the position of a room on one of
the upper tiers. In that room is a certain prisoner, whom
you will slay. The red dotted line indicates the route you
will follow to and from the target chamber. Memorize the
plan well."

I did so, having been trained in the arts of memory as
well as murder. Not that I intended murdering anyone for
Gurjan Tor, of course. Once free of this building, I would
go about my own business, and the lords of The World
Above have pity on the souls of any Assassins who tried
to get in my way!

"The second red cross on the higher level indicates the
chamber wherein a second prisoner is immured. This
prisoner, too, you will slay. The weapon of choice for
both deeds is the needle-stiletto in whose use Klygon in-
forms me you have been trained to excellence. On this occasion, a mere scratch will suffice, for the blade has been
steeped in *phuol*-venom."

"And who are these two prisoners I am to murder, if I
may ask?" I inquired, greatly daring.

Gurjan Tor studied me thoughtfully for a few moments,
then shrugged fat quivering shoulders.

"No reason why you should not know," he said. "The
second prisoner is a strange winged golden-skinned male
creature with violet eyes whom the archpriestess is passing
off on a deluded and superstitious populace as a blessed
amphashand."

I reeled. Then Gurjan Tor dropped a second bombshell.

"The first prisoner is Niamh the Fair, regnant Princess
of Phaolon, whom Arjala holds as a means of controlling
Akhmim."

And then he dropped the third.

"Klygon will accompany you on this mission to see that you do not stray from the appointed task. If you do, he will kill you. . . ."

Chapter 25

PROJECT THREE

My mind in a whirl, I followed Klygon from the room and went with him to the floor where the novices were housed and trained.

Now the full scheme had been made known to me, I understood the thinking of Gurjan Tor in all its insidious complexity. Arjala's hold over the Tyrant of Ardha lay in her possession of Niamh. With Niamh slain in the Temple itself, a new breech would widen between the two factions. Moreover, Gurjan Tor's agents would doubtless spread it about that Arjala had ordered the Princess of Phaolon murdered, which would further enrage Akhmim and might cause considerable resentment among the citizenry to boot, since Niamh was a valuable captive worth an enormous ransom.

As for Zarqa, I had at this time no idea how he had come to fall into Arjala's toils, but the chief of the Assassins had said something about her passing him off as one of the mythical winged messengers from the Laonese heaven, so his murder would probably be considered the ultimate limit in sacrilege.

So it turned out that Project Three actually fitted in with my own most earnest wishes to a remarkable degree! The Assassins would somehow get me into the Temple, thus affording me the perfect opportunity to free the woman I loved and my sad-eyed Kalood friend, as well. It could not have been more ideal for my purposes if I had designed the scheme myself.

That my ugly little mentor and friend Klygon would accompany me on this mission was the only element in the plan I regretted. I had become enormously fond of the homely, humorous little man in the days just past, and I had no desire to injure his standing with his chief—and certainly no wish to kill him. But I could hardly permit this sentiment to stand in the way of the safety of the woman I loved. No, Klygon would be gotten out of the way, somehow.

We napped, rose, bathed, feasted lightly, and armed ourselves for the fulfillment of Project Three. For the first and, I hoped, the last time, I donned the skintight black raiment of the Assassins. I slung the coil of Live Rope around my shoulders, hid the vial of Liquid Flame in the purse at my girdle, and clipped the scabbards which held the poisoned stiletto and a slender, well-balanced long sword to the warriors' harness of black leather straps I had donned over my Assassins' raiment. As I settled the customary black silk visor over my face, I reflected on the events to come. It was going to be quite a night!

But just what kind of a night, I had no slightest inkling.

The house of Gurjan Tor rose on the outskirts of Ardha, in a dingy and furtive quarter of the city, given over to crooked alleys, grimy wineshops, slums, and hovels.

We ascended by curving ramps to the roof of the building. There rose covered pens in which *zaiphs* and *dhua* were tethered. For our purpose, Klygon had selected two especially trained *zaiphs*. I have elsewhere in these chronicles had occasion to describe the peculiar flying steeds used by the Laonese in lieu of horses. They resemble nothing so much as mailed and glittering dragonflies grown to the size of Percherons. Because of their sparkling, transparent wings and glistening armor-like chitin, you might think them an odd choice for a night mission of the greatest stealth and secrecy, since the slightest glimmer of reflection could easily betray our position to watchful guards. Well, the astute Klygon had anticipated this, and the twin *zaiphs* he had chosen for our steeds had been painted on their horny parts with a dull, nonreflecting tarry substance. As for their oval, elongated, glassy wings, these had been dulled and darkened with sooty powder.

We mounted the saddles strapped about the upper thorax of our winged steeds. I gathered the reins in my hand as the *zaiph*-keepers strapped us in against danger of falling. There came the humming thunder of beating wings. The enormous insects rose from the roof, circled the house of Gurjan Tor once, and they soared off through the night sky in the direction of the Temple precinct.

We did not permit our *zaiphs* to perch on the Temple roof, for here the Temple Guards kept their own *zaiphs* penned and the usual keepers were doubtless about; we could hardly have landed without protection. Instead, we guided our mounts to the level above that described by Gurjan Tor as the apartment in which Zarqa the Kalood was imprisoned. Then the *zaiphs* hovered on throbbing vans while Klygon and I unstrapped ourselves from the saddles and climbed out onto the face of the building. The ornamental sculpture wherewith the Laonese customarily adorn their buildings, sometimes to the point of excess, naturally afforded us a variety of hand- and footholds. Thus neither Klygon nor I found it particularly difficult to climb down the outer wall to a ledge whereon we could stand erect.

As we slithered down the wall toward the ledge, I reflected wryly yet again on the fortunate fact that the Laonese do not suffer from the fear of heights; for what I was then engaged in doing—creeping down the sheer face of a building hundreds of feet above the pavement, clinging by my fingers and toes alone—would have petrified most Earthmen with utter terror.

We gained the ledge in safety and I secured one end of my Live Rope about a heavy caryatid and let the line dangle down to the window of Niamh's suite.

As I did so I heard a muffled explosion, followed by a shrill cry of fear.

I climbed over the ledge on my belly and seized hold of the line, thinking nothing in particular about the sounds I had heard. Just then my thoughts were filled with the problem of Klygon and how to rid myself of his presence without having to kill him. I was also preoccupied with the problem of clambering down the line, for the Live Rope we had taken from Sarchimus' tower was slick and glassy and not easy to get a grip on.

Then a ruddy light steamed through the window below my heels and I heard the crackle of flames!

I didn't have the slightest idea what was going on in Niamh's suite, but it was obvious some kind of accident had occureed and the possibility that my beloved was in danger spurred me to new feats of agility.

I clambered further down the line toward her window, through which flames now crackled.

Above me on the edge, Klygon knelt, steadying the line.

And then there occurred the most incredible and unexpected sequence of events imaginable. So swiftly did it happen that it was over in seconds, and there was a dreamlike unreality about it all.

As I clung to the line, descending toward Niamh's window, but still some yards above it, invisible in my black cloak and garments against view from below, something came hurtling out of the night to hover before the window which was my goal.

It was the sky-sled, with Zarqa mounted upon it!

The sled came to a stop before the window and the gaunt Kalood reached across the sill to touch someone on the shoulder, and I heard a woman scream.

A fraction of a second later the arms of a stalwart young man appeared, lifting the slim body of a girl out onto the sled.

The girl was Niamh!

A moment later, the young man—Prince Janchan—appeared in the window bearing an uconscious woman of remarkable and vivid beauty. From the gemmed coronet and breastplates and girdle she wore, I was certain she could be none other than Arjala herself.

He lifted her into the waiting arms of Zarqa, who deposited her beside Niamh in the rear of the sled.

Then he sprang from the inferno the room had swiftly become and clambered upon the sled himself.

And, so swiftly had all of this taken place, that still I hung there, clinging to the line, frozen with shock, unable to speak or move or even to cry out.

And in the very next instant the sled swung away, bearing left, and flashed from sight.

I hung there helplessly, as Zarqa the Kalood and Prince Janchan flew to safety, bearing away Niamh the Fair—leaving me behind, dangling far above the street, at the mercy of the Assassins, in the city of my enemies in which I no longer had one single friend!

Editor's Note

The First National Bank of Harritton, Connecticut, holds in its vaults a safe deposit box registered in the name of one of the oldest and most distinguished families of the state. Upon the demise of the last surviving member of this family, pursuant to instructions written into his will, the box was opened by three senior members of the legal firm of Brinton, Brinton, and Carruthers, who discovered therein a number of manuscript journals.

These manuscripts related a narrative of marvels and adventures upon a remote world. Although told in the first person, they were of so fantastic a nature that the lawyers were reluctant to release them for publication, as the will clearly stipulated. I suspect the reason for this reluctance on the part of the lawyers was that if the documents were accepted on face value the weird and uncanny narrative might throw suspicion upon the sanity of their author, which could throw into dispute the divisions of his property as set forth in the will; but this is only a guess on my part.

It was the younger son of the senior member of the firm who brought me into the picture. I had met this young man at several science fiction conventions in Baltimore, Philadelphia, and New York, and know him as an enthusiast of fantasy in general and of my own novels and stories in particular. He persuaded his father to arrange a meeting with me at my Long Island home where the details of a peculiar arrangement were discussed and the manuscripts were given into my possession.

This young man (whom I will call Tom Anderson, although that is not his name) was well aware of my anomalous position in the genre of imaginative fiction. That is, not only am I an author, but also an editor of fantasy.

174

In my editorial capacity, it was thought I might well arrange the publications of the journals. Brinton, Brinton, and Carruthers had no objection to releasing the journals for publication but desired that the family name should be kept out of the picture. The family is one of the oldest in Connecticut and has given two governors and three senators to the state, and so distinguished and reputable a name, it was thought, should not be linked with novels of such extravagant imagination.

My connection with these books, then, has simply been that of an editor. My publisher, Mr. Donald A. Wollheim, quite naturally assumes me to have written them myself, despite my protestations. But since I am not permitted to attach the name of the actual author to these fictions, there was nothing else to do but attach my own. This afterword is by way of acknowledging credit where credit is due.

In assembling the manuscripts for publication, I have found the chief difficulty one of length. The journals simply run on and on, forming one continuous story. This factor alone, by the way, nearly convinces me of the veracity of the narrative, for in real life adventures do not come to a neat and final conclusion at the termination of sixty thousand words. The interminable structure of the story, however, presents considerable hazards to the unfortunate reader. In the present book, for instance. the narrative ends at a point of high suspense and leaves the central problems of the plot completely unresolved. In the parlance of the old movie adventure serials I loved in my youth, you might call this ending a cliff-hanger to end all cliff-hangers.

But I have no other recourse than to end the story at this point, for sixty thousand words is sixty thousand words, and I have neither the permission of the author's estate nor any personal inclination to tamper drastically with the literary work of another man.

For the unfortunate reader, thus left hanging, as it were, I believe I can offer some slight amelioration of his uncomfortable position. While I have yet to penetrate very deeply into the unpublished portions of the narrative—which is in longhand, by the way, and has to be laboriously and slowly rendered into typescript—and while I myself do not as yet know how the story ends, it should be quite obvious that Karn escapes from the predicaments in which we left him a few pages ago, else we should never have had these journals to read. And, since the various adventures of Zarqa the Kalood and of Prince Janchan of Phaolon happened "offstage," as it were, and without the participation or witness of Karn, the narrator, it becomes perfectly obvious that at some future point in the unpublished portion of these journals he rejoined his friends, whom we last saw flying off on the sky-sled, leaving him behind. If he is not to rejoin them at a future point in the narrative, how, then, could he possibly have learned of the adventures which befell them after they became separated?

But I'm afraid this is all that can at present be conjectured concerning the remainder of the story. There are many projects, both auctorial and editorial, which are clamoring for my immediate attention. And it will be some time before I have sufficient leisure to begin my explorations of the unpublished remainder of the journals.

We shall have to wait and see how the story ends, you and I.

—LIN CARTER

Hollis, Long Island, New York